A River
TO CROSS

Books by Yvonne Harris

The Vigilante's Bride
A River to Cross

A River TO CROSS

YVONNE HARRIS

BETHANY HOUSE PUBLISHERS
a division of Baker Publishing Group
Minneapolis, Minnesota

Cover design by John Hamilton Design
Cover photography © Getty Images

Published by Bethany House Publishers
11400 Hampshire Avenue South
Bloomington, Minnesota 55438
www.bethanyhouse.com

Bethany House Publishers is a division of
Baker Publishing Group, Grand Rapids, Michigan

Printed in the United States of America

Library of Congress Cataloging-in-Publication Data
Harris, Yvonne L.
    A river to cross / Yvonne Harris.
        p.   cm.
    ISBN 978-0-7642-0805-8 (pbk.)
    1. Texas Rangers—Fiction. 2. Texas—History—1846–1950—Fiction.
3. Mexican-American Border Region—Fiction. I. Title.
PS3608.A78329R58 2011
813′.6—dc22   2011019407

Scripture quotations are from the King James Version of the Bible.

11 12 13 14 15 16 17   7 6 5 4 3 2 1

For Robert, again

One

ELIZABETH EVANS LIFTED HER SKIRTS and sprinted up the back stairs of the courthouse. At the third-floor landing she hauled open the heavy door and propped it with her hip. Grinning, she called down to her brother, puffing up the steps. "I don't believe it. You can't keep up with me, Lloyd."

"It's ninety-eight degrees outside, and I'm ten years older than you." Flushed and out of breath, Lloyd Madison frowned at the small woman in ruffled green silk and trudged up the last few steps to the landing. He took her elbow and steered her into a long, windowed corridor with a pair of tall hammered brass doors at the end.

Lloyd pointed to the silent elevator. The clock above it said 11:10.

"A few more minutes and that elevator would've been fixed, and we could've ridden up like normal people," he said.

Elizabeth let out a little hoot of laughter. "Ha, not with Mexico right across the river. In this part of the world, a few minutes means tomorrow or next week. Besides, only an idiot would ride up in that rickety birdcage you call an elevator."

Lloyd laughed and threw an arm around her. "Hush now. It's modern and it's perfectly safe. The town spent a lot of money on that elevator, and it's only nervous Nellies like you who won't ride in it." He hugged her. "You little skeptic. My readers are going to love you. You're on their side already."

A guilty grin burst across her face. "You picked that up fast," she said, laughing.

"I run a newspaper, remember? That's my job."

When they were younger, she'd always looked up to him. Now, in one of life's turnabouts, she was looking *after* him and his three-year-old daughter, Ruthie. When his wife and newborn son died last spring, Lloyd asked Elizabeth to come live with them in El Paso after she graduated from college. He needed family to help him get his life in order. In return, he offered to teach her the newspaper business. He owned and operated the *Grande Examiner*, El Paso's leading newspaper.

Elizabeth was tempted. From time to time she'd written gossipy "Inside Washington" pieces for his paper under a male pseudonym, and they were a big hit with El Paso readers.

"School's over; you've got your degree, so tomorrow you're going to come work for me. Right?" her father asked over dinner the day she graduated.

She laid her napkin down. "I don't think so, Daddy. I tried that last summer, remember?"

Carlton Madison, U.S. Senior Senator from Texas, had squired her around to lunch all over Washington and lied through his teeth, telling her and everyone else how important she was, while all she did was make his coffee. He loved her. He just wanted her around.

"I've been thinking. How about I make you my speechwriter this time?" he said. "Would you like that?"

She let out a long sigh and got out of her chair. She walked over and kissed him soundly on the cheek, then went upstairs to her room and started packing for Texas.

But writing for Texans was one thing, she thought, stacking petticoats and chemises in a small calfskin traveling trunk. Moving out there was quite another. Just the thought of leaving Washington with its theaters and shops and elegant restaurants for Texas with its rough countryside and even rougher men made her uneasy.

That was silly, she told herself. Fort Bliss was almost next door. With the U.S. Army a mere three miles away, El Paso was probably the safest place in all of Texas.

In the courthouse, she pointed to the double doors at the end of the corridor. "How long will this meeting take?"

Lloyd shrugged. "Hard to say. People want to know why I wrote that the stepped-up border raids by Mexican bandits are an attempt to draw the U.S. into war with Mexico."

"How did you find *that* out?" she asked.

"Took me a while," Lloyd said with a sour smile, "but I finally have a good source in Mexico. Had to put pressure on a Ranger captain to get it—and pushing those guys around is never a good idea. This one runs a Ranger company for the Frontier Battalion out of Camp Annex, a former subpost of

Fort Bliss. He refused to talk to me without both Federal and state approval."

Lloyd laughed and shook his head. "Me—the son of a United States senator—and I had to get Washington's permission to talk to him."

"Did he help?"

"I'll say. And he knows a lot more than he's telling me. Mexican Army General Manuel Diego is a military thug and a liar. He wants to push President Guevara out. Says Guevara is a lackey of the United States. Not true. Guevara's a friend and ally. And it's been a long time since we had anyone in Mexico we could call a friend."

"You already knew that, though."

"Yes and no. The captain warned me to go easy with Diego, said however much we dislike the little general, Diego has a lot of support, and he just might win. Good advice, but I didn't want to hear it."

"Could he be wrong?"

Lloyd looked at her for a moment, then shook his head thoughtfully. "I doubt it. This man doesn't make mistakes. When the captain was in the Army, he was in Fourth Cavalry reconnaissance, so I figure he ought to know." Lloyd smiled down at her. "Actually, I'd like you to meet him."

Elizabeth held a hand up. "Thanks, but I'll pass. Carl was in the Cavalry. And if I remember correctly, *reconnaissance* is a nice euphemism for *spy*."

Lloyd chuckled and squeezed her shoulder. "I really don't think he's a spy. In fact, he isn't in the Army anymore. The Frontier Battalion went after him and wooed him over to their side. He's a Texas Ranger now."

"A Texas Ranger? Good grief, Lloyd, keep him away from me."

"Keep an open mind, Elizabeth. You're young, pretty. Ought to be out having a good time and thinking about getting married again. Instead, you hardly ever go out, and when you do, the men have slicked up hair and smell prettier than you. Fort Bliss has a hundred *real* men out there you could meet."

"No thanks," she said.

Lloyd frowned at her. "You're passing up some of the best men in the world. What have you got against the military?"

"Not a thing," Elizabeth answered quickly. "If I did, I wouldn't come out here to live. I love my country. I'm proud of it, proud of you. I loved Carl, and I'll never forget him. But I don't love the Army, and I'm not marrying another man who does."

"But why?" Lloyd asked.

"In the military, the wife comes second. Duty comes first." Her face tightened. "Carl was killed doing his duty."

Lloyd shook his head. "Carl was a hero. He was killed in an Indian attack, what he joined the service to prevent. What happened to him wasn't the Army's fault. If we're going to have a country that can hold its own in the world, it has to be a place that's safe to live and work and go to school in. We need a strong Army with a big fist. El Paso has that with Fort Bliss. But you're never going to give the Army a chance again because it might end in pain for you. Is that it?"

She smiled and hugged him. "You got it. It's called survival, Lloyd."

Lloyd grabbed the heavy brass door handles, opened the

door, and edged her inside ahead of him. "And you know I'm going to change your mind!"

"Lloyd, wait!" Sheriff Bud Wagner, a balding middle-aged man she'd met before, hurried over. He touched the brim of his hat and gave a slight bow to Elizabeth.

"Hey, Bud." Lloyd shook the sheriff's hand warmly. "I came in early today to talk to you, but got held up outside with neighbors wanting to meet Elizabeth. How about after the meeting, maybe over coffee?" Lloyd said, and added quietly, "I have some new information for you about these border raids."

"Coffee sounds good. See any seats, Miz Evans?"

Up on her toes, Elizabeth pointed to several empty seats down front. Tugging Lloyd's arm, she started down the aisle, Sheriff Wagner close behind.

It appeared as if everyone from the local seamstress to the bank president was there. Her chest tightened with pride for her brother. Alarmed about the surge in Mexican outlaws crossing over and cattle theft around El Paso, the whole town had come to hear Lloyd talk.

∞

"Order. Order. The house will be in order!"

On the dais at the front of the room, El Paso's Mayor Bob Jackson gaveled for silence. The vaulted rotunda with its encircling visitors' gallery quieted as the clerk began to call the roll.

Elizabeth opened her reticule and took out a pencil and small notebook. She flipped to a blank page and waited, ready to take notes for a follow-up article. She was fairly itching to get into it. This one had a real story.

The chamber quieted as the chaplain began his opening prayer. As heads bowed, a hush settled over the room. "Dear Lord in heaven, we thank you for this meeting and for the many councilmen at this table and the good works they and our citizens are doing in El Paso. We thank you for guiding us in our decision making and showing us the way to—"

The double brass doors at the back of the room crashed open against the walls.

"Nobody moves, nobody gets hurt!" shouted a man with a heavy Mexican accent.

Soldiers in blue uniforms with white straps crisscrossing their chests jumped through the doorway. Legs braced, they stationed themselves against the walls and aimed their weapons at the dais and the members of the El Paso City Council.

Elizabeth grabbed Lloyd's hand. "Who—?"

"They're Mexican Army, and they want to be sure we know it," he whispered. "The officer in charge is Major Chavez. I met him a year ago. I remember that scarred cheek of his."

The major stood in the doorway. Beneath the small red cap he wore, a clipped dark beard hid the lower part of his face. Scowling, he strode toward the dais and turned to face the room, legs spread.

A thick silence charged the room.

The major looked out over the semicircular rows of benches and the frightened faces of the audience.

He moved his head in little jerks like a puppet, looking for someone. Then he snapped his hand up and pointed directly at Lloyd.

"Ah, Señor Madison, you will come with me, please."

Elizabeth sucked in a quiet hiss of surprise.

Lloyd stiffened. "What's the meaning of this, Major?"

"We have much to talk about." Unhurriedly, Chavez drew a heavy black pistol from a side holster. Staring at Lloyd, he thumbed the hammer back. The two clicks cocking the revolver were unmistakable.

Elizabeth clenched her hands, her eyes fixed on the major. The scar down the side of his face had turned an angry, dusky red. In the stillness she was aware of dozens of eyes fixed on Lloyd and her.

Chavez stroked his thumb back and forth along the trigger guard of the pistol. "Señor, you come with me or I shoot. You choose."

The councilmen exchanged worried looks.

White-faced, Lloyd rose slowly and moved toward the end of the row.

Elizabeth grabbed his sleeve as he pushed by. "Lloyd, no! Please don't go," she said.

He patted her hand. "Don't worry. It's probably all a mistake. I'll talk to him and see what's going on."

Chavez looked at his men, then at Lloyd, and pointed to the doors.

Lloyd walked stiffly ahead of Chavez toward the back of the room. As soon as they turned into the hall, a scuffle broke out.

Deep shouts.

A burst of gunshots sounded.

Sheriff Wagner leaped into the aisle and bolted for the doors, his pistol drawn. When he had disappeared into the hall, the loud crack of a rifle rang out. And then another.

Elizabeth drove to her feet and pushed past the knees of two older women sitting alongside her.

"Help them!" she yelled to the men on the stage. Grabbing her skirts up with both hands, she broke into a hard run for the doors to the hall.

"Stop her!" a male voice cried out.

Councilmen rushed from the dais to join her, pulling their pistols as they did. She blinked in surprise. Half the men on that stage were armed. Running, shouting, they surged into the corridor after her and ran into the middle of a small war.

More shots.

The triple stained-glass windows overlooking the Rio Grande in the distance blew out with a *blam*! She threw herself against the wall.

Boots, rifles, uniforms blurred past. Running councilmen shooting at soldiers, and soldiers shooting back. Bullets whined. Smoking black holes blew across the ceiling.

Three soldiers lay in the hall. Seven others bolted for the stairway, chased by the councilmen behind, firing at them. Sheriff Wagner, shot in the leg, leaned against the wall and aimed at a soldier running past. His mouth tightened when the man staggered and fell.

"Go!" Chavez shouted, pointing down the hall.

Elizabeth snapped her head around. The major was running alone.

"Lloyd!" she cried. *Dear God, where is he?*

There! Halfway down the hall, Lloyd and a Mexican soldier lay sprawled facedown on the floor, unmoving. Icy coldness spread through her chest as she ran toward him. She dropped to her knees in the hall beside him and grabbed his shoulder to roll him over.

Please, God, don't let him be dead. Please ...

Her mouth twisted silently, and she knew he was gone, killed by one of the soldiers.

Stunned by what was happening, she looked around, took in the chaos in the hall, the haze of blue smoke, the noise.

Knees pumping, Major Chavez pounded after his soldiers for the stairway at the end of the hall. Mid-stride, he changed direction and reached his left arm at her. In one blinding instant she knew what he was going to do.

She jumped to her feet and spun around to run. A heavy arm grabbed her.

As he bore down on her, her gaze shot to his scarred cheek. She threw her hands up to ward him off, but he yanked her against him and crooked his arm around her throat. Using her as a shield, he held her in front of him and dragged her backward down the hall. High heels slipping on the polished floor, she clawed at his arm and tried to scream. No sound came out.

Fear had dried up her throat.

Chavez jammed the pistol barrel against her neck.

"Stay back!" he yelled to the councilmen.

The mayor wheeled around. "Hold your fire!" he shouted to the councilmen behind.

Elizabeth wrenched away from the major, but tripped and stumbled to her knees. Ears ringing from the shots, she crawled against the wall. The hall reeked of spent gunpowder.

Chavez grabbed her up again, threw her over his shoulder like a sack of flour, and ducked into the stairwell. Two at a time, he leaped down the steps.

Hanging down his back, Elizabeth got a mouthful of

air and found her voice. Kicking, screaming, she beat him with both fists.

"Let me go! Let me go!"

He kicked the outside door open and ran around the building to the hitching rails. The six soldiers who had escaped ahead of him were already on their horses and racing down the grassy slope for the National Freight Yards and the Rio Grande beyond.

With Elizabeth over his shoulder, Chavez hauled himself into the saddle. He slammed her down hard in front of him and spurred the horse into a flying gallop for the river. They tore across the street, down the slope, and into the busy freight yards.

A whistle shrieked.

A bell *clang-clang-clang*ed like doomsday.

Elizabeth's mouth fell open in a scream of terror.

Smoke pouring, sparks flying, a big black locomotive barreled down on them.

She was still screaming as Chavez raced across the tracks in front of the train, shouting to the horse, "Go! Go! Go!"

Two

18 Miles South of Fort Bliss

"Hey, Captain! Hold on a minute!"

The horseman's voice cut through the thin air of the Texas desert, then faded quickly, the sound soaked up by the heat. A cloud of pinkish dust swirled behind him.

Jake Nelson lifted a hand and halted the team of men with him. He reined his horse to a stop near a stand of willow trees around a trickle of water. Not much of a stream, he thought, but enough for the horses and a little shade for the men.

The landscape of flat red dirt and broken rock shimmered in the heat. Jake raised his head when the rider called again, flailing his mount to run faster.

Sergeant Gus Dukker, straddling a big black and white Appaloosa, shielded his eyes and watched the rider. "He should know better. It's too hot to ride a horse that way," he said. "Who is that idiot?"

Jake grinned. "Must be an officer. Can't tell yet; too far

away, but he's in uniform, which means he's one of ours, so I'd rather you didn't shoot him."

An undercurrent of laughter rippled through the other men.

"I saw the uniform too, and that only makes it worse," Gus said. He took off his wide-brimmed hat, smoothed a dark patch of hair from his forehead, and pulled his hat back on. "The uniform guarantees whatever he wants from us, we ain't gonna like it."

"You're probably right there. Still, we don't look all that official ourselves. Maybe we should button our shirts."

Gus snorted. "You first, boss."

Jake looked as scruffy as they did. Perspiration slicked his face, and his shirt hung open, his chest sandy and sticky with sweat. But it was hot and a long-sleeved open shirt was almost standard. It looked sloppy, yet it allowed air to circulate while protecting them from the sun—important for him with his light hair, and for Fred Barkley, the redhead alongside Jake.

They were Rangers, part of the new Frontier Battalion charged with restoring law and order to Texas. Since they were considered the cream of the military, they dressed any way they pleased. They did not wear uniforms and were proud of it. Halfway between an army and a police force, they had nearly unlimited authority, including the power of arrest.

Though not U.S. Army, sometimes they worked together. Before they joined the Texas Rangers, Jake and several of his men had been members of the Fourth U.S. Cavalry and had worn uniforms identical to the one coming toward them. Since the approaching rider was wearing the same, Jake figured he was from Fort Bliss, eighteen miles north.

The military complex of Fort Bliss and the adjoining sub-post lay three miles outside El Paso. Camp Annex had been a small U.S. Cavalry post thirty years ago when Indians were a problem. Once that lessened, the Army expanded Fort Bliss and abandoned Camp Annex and its half dozen buildings.

But the Texas Rangers saw the adobe and log buildings as infinitely better than their tents. They grabbed up hammers and saws and moved in with the blessing of Fort Bliss. There was now a good lane that connected the two. Relations were cordial and cooperative. Camp Annex provided extra stable facilities when Fort Bliss was full.

A few minutes later, sides heaving, the horse racing toward them plunged to a stop and its rider dismounted. He walked to Jake, snapped to attention, and saluted.

Jake returned the salute and swung off his horse. "Relax, Lieutenant, we're not very formal out here." He stuck out his hand. "I'm Captain Jake Nelson. What can we do for you?"

"Lieutenant Taylor, sir," he said, and handed Jake a small yellow envelope. "Colonel Gordon got the same telegram this morning from the adjutant general—"

Jake's head snapped up. "Which adjutant general, Washington or Austin?"

"Both, sir. State and Federal."

Definitely not good. Jake kept his face blank and ripped open the envelope. With both adjutant generals on it, there was a problem somewhere—a big problem. He took out a single yellow sheet and read it. He swore softly.

"Mexicans, again." He handed the telegram up to Gus, who read it and then passed it around to the other men.

"Told you we weren't gonna like it," Gus said, shaking his head.

"Looks like Senator Madison got wind of trouble from Mexico heading for his son Lloyd out here," Jake said. "Some of you haven't met him yet, but Lloyd runs the newspaper in El Paso and prints all of General Diego's dirty little plans. Nice man, smart, honest, and Texan to the core. Apparently, Diego doesn't like that and wants Madison and his paper—the *Grande Examiner*—shut down. Permanently."

"Shut down? You mean assassinated?" Gus asked.

"Reads that way to me," Jake said.

The faces looking back at him were stone-hard. His men were Texas lawmen as well as Texas Rangers.

Jake shook his head. Confrontations with Mexican bandits were ramping up. Almost nightly the bandits slipped over the border and terrorized Texas settlers. Murder, rape, and stealing cattle were common. General Manuel Diego was trying to goad the U.S. to retaliate.

In the last ten days, Jake and his team had been in shootouts with four separate groups of bandits. As usual, the Mexicans ran for the border whenever the Rangers appeared.

And the U.S. Army was forbidden to go into Mexico after them.

Even so, the Rangers shot at them in the river before they could reach the other side. They'd chased into the water after them and tried to turn them back. Horses rearing, neighing, splashing, they fired with everything they had—pistols, rifles, shotguns—because once the Mexicans made it to their side of the Rio Grande, they were safe.

The boundary between Mexico and the United States kept changing. Officially, the international boundary was the center of the deepest channel of the Rio Grande. Since the river changed channels, dug new ones or dried up, depending on the season, the boundary was hard to determine. It frequently overflowed its banks, adversely affecting crops and homes and animals. Rangers had to settle for not setting foot on the Mexican bank.

Jake followed the order to the letter. Most of the time. Teams of Texas Rangers invading Mexico and shooting Mexicans on their own soil would be a serious international violation, a provocation that could lead to war. Nobody wanted another war with Mexico.

Except General Diego. The turmoil even a small war would create would make it easier for him to oust the current president and take over himself. He'd been stirring up trouble on both sides of the border for over a year.

One of the men passed the yellow telegram back to Jake. Standing close by, Gus asked, "How we gonna do this, Jake? We're not due back on post till next week."

Inside, Jake's stomach tightened—a sixth-sense stirring almost too faint to recognize—warning him that time was a factor, and it was running out. And hard experience had taught him that sometimes his brain got it wrong. But his gut? Never.

He glanced at the sun directly overhead. "We can't wait; we're going back now. Let's finish here and get started. If we hurry, we can be at Madison's by three o'clock."

Jake swung himself back into the saddle and turned his horse. "Lieutenant, you're welcome to ride with us and take a personal report back for Colonel Gordon. The sooner Lloyd Madison knows what we do, the better."

Three

The Madison Ranch

It was midafternoon when Jake pointed to the open gate and white-fenced lane leading to Madison's house, a large white Colonial with a wraparound porch. It was a rich man's house, a two-story, and set well back off the road. He'd been there to dinner with Lloyd several times.

"That's it," he said, frowning, studying the chimney. Odd. No smoke.

As they rode toward the house, he noticed an unusual number of birds. They were everywhere. Eleven turkey buzzards coasted on the updrafts high over a barn beyond the house. The hair prickled on the back of his neck. A dozen more of the big black birds hunched in the trees around the barn.

"Something big must've died out here to attract that many," he said. Chills ran down his back, and he rolled his shoulders to chase them. With their thick beaks and rubbery necks, he thought vultures were the ugliest wild things in nature.

Talking among themselves, the men rode closer. When they got to the corral, all conversation stopped. The gate was wide open. Inside, three dead horses, two dogs, and a dozen chickens lay in the corral, all recently shot.

Sickened, Jake slid off his horse. Gun drawn, he started for the open barn. "Let's check inside." Three Rangers climbed off their horses and joined him. The others walked their horses off to the side and pulled their rifles.

In the Cavalry, he'd been in Reconnaissance and had specialized in silent approaches and elimination of sentries. In the Frontier Battalion, he trained his men in the same techniques. As Rangers, they handled weapons better than almost anyone and were lethal in hand-to-hand fighting.

Those reports he'd written on reducing casualties by using the more highly trained Ranger teams instead of regular Rangers caught someone's attention in Austin. Adjutant General Wilburn King, Frontier Battalion commander, pulled Jake and six Ranger companies out of the Nueces Strip and sent them to El Paso on the Mexican border to put a stop to the ongoing incursions there.

When it came to carrying out operations, Jake was a planner. He'd learned from experience that most plans go wrong. Because of his insistence on double backups, his Rangers had acquired a reputation for surviving all odds. It had reached the point that if the Battalion needed something done quick and dirty, they asked for one of Nelson's teams.

He had an uneasy feeling this was going to be another one.

"Captain, can you use one more in the barn?" the lieutenant called.

Jake looked back and saw the eagerness in the young

officer's eyes. Twelve years earlier, Private Jake Nelson, a big fifteen-year-old kid who had lied about his age to join up, would've asked the same question.

He swept his hand. "Sure can. Bring your rifle, Lieutenant, and come on."

When they came out of the barn a few minutes later, Jake stood in the middle of the corral, hands on his hips. He looked around at the well-kept ranch, the white rail fences around the pasture and the big barn. "Something is very wrong here," he said. "Barn's empty. Horses and dogs killed, gates open, and no one's come out to see who we are."

"Maybe they're not home," the lieutenant said.

Gus gave him a hard look. "Or maybe they were."

Jake shrugged off his striped vest. "Don't know what we're going to run into here. So let's look like what we are." He buttoned his dusty white shirt up the front, tucked it in his trousers, and pulled on a black necktie. He shrugged his vest back on, the pockets bulging with bullets.

Ten Rangers and Lieutenant Taylor, who had long since shucked his uniform jacket and opened his own shirt, like the Rangers, dismounted and put themselves back together. They tied the horses to a hitching rail a short distance from the house. Pistols in hand, they spread out and approached the white house.

Without a word they separated and surrounded the house. Alert for anything out of the ordinary, Jake and Fred Barkley walked up the steps to the front porch. Standing off to the side, Jake leaned over and beat on the door.

No answer. He pounded the door again.

"Texas Rangers, open up!"

No answer.

He drew his knee up and kicked the door open.

The room was empty and had been vandalized. Sofa cushions lay strewn about the living room, chairs overturned, and every lamp in sight had been smashed. Some thrown against the wall. Broken glass covered the floor.

On their way to the kitchen, they checked the other rooms downstairs. A large house, it had a spacious dining room, an office, and a library with a piano. Many of its keys were broken, hit with something heavy. He pressed a key, the single note clear and sounding unusually loud in the silence.

In the kitchen, they let the others in through a side door. Remembering the smokeless chimney he'd seen from the road, Jake ran his hand over the top of the cast-iron cookstove. Cold.

"Whatever happened here happened hours ago," he said. Doubting he would get any kind of response, he called, "Hello, hello. Anybody home?"

A high-pitched shriek from upstairs answered him.

"Daddy, Daddy, come get me!"

Three men broke for the stairs.

Upstairs in a child's room, a little girl about three years old, tears streaming down her face, lay in a corner, sobbing, her hands and feet bound behind her. The small bed was torn apart, mattress and blankets tossed on the floor.

Jake set an overturned chair upright, then lifted her, and sat with her on his lap. Stroking her hair, he tried to calm her.

"Your daddy's not here right now, but it's all right, Ruthie," he said, and steadied her elbows while Fred untied her wrists and ankles.

"Is Miz Annie here with you?" he asked her.

She nodded. "Yeth," she lisped, and pointed to the hall.

"Jake, in here," Gus called from a bedroom at the far end of the hall. "We found the housekeeper. She says Mexican soldiers broke in the house late this morning. She and the little girl are the only ones here. We're untying her now."

Jake, carrying Ruthie, her little arms clenched tight around his neck, walked down the hall, his heavy boots rapping the oak floor. From the doorway he looked in at the housekeeper. "They tore this room up, too." Clothes were strewn on the floor, the wardrobes emptied.

"Miz Annie, you need a doctor?" he asked.

"Oh, Captain Nelson, thank God you're here. I think we're all right. The soldiers were in such a rush to get out, they didn't touch me or Ruthie."

"She seems fine. If she'd been hurt by a strange man today, she wouldn't act like this. She won't let me put her down. But then she knows me. Still, just to be safe, I want you both to see the doc."

Later, in the dining room downstairs, Annie brought Ruthie a sandwich and a glass of milk and sat beside her at the table. Annie told them that ten soldiers forced their way into the house, demanding to see Lloyd.

"What color uniforms?" Jake broke in.

"Blue and white, with red neck scarves. They sounded Mexican."

"They probably were."

"When I told them Lloyd wasn't home, they didn't believe me and went all through the house yelling and throwing the furniture around. Not until they threatened to take Ruthie with them did I tell them Lloyd was at the courthouse in town."

She drained her own glass and set it down. "He was giving

a speech this morning. He and Elizabeth left early so they could talk to the sheriff before the meeting."

Jake's eyebrows pulled together. "Who's Elizabeth?"

"His younger sister," Annie said. "She arrived from Washington last week."

"He mentioned he had a sister, but I don't recall he said she was coming to Texas."

Annie's expression softened. "She and Lloyd are close. She came out here to look after him. When his wife died last year, Lloyd asked her to come live with him when she finished school. She's a writer, and he needs family to help him get his life in order. In return, he's teaching her the newspaper business."

Ruthie slid off her chair and ran across the room to a group of family photographs on a mahogany chest by the window. She snatched up a small oval frame, ran back, and climbed up into Jake's lap. She handed it to him.

When Jake glanced down at it, his heart gave a funny little bump that surprised him. "Who's this?"

"Aunt 'Lithabeth. Daddy says she's boo-ful."

Boo-ful.

Her daddy was right. She certainly was.

A dark-haired young woman with laughing eyes and dimples smiled up at him—pretty. Nice, very nice. But then he always did have a weakness for long hair. He shook his head. Pretty as she was, he had no time for women now. Certainly not her kind. Elizabeth was a lady, a senator's daughter. He smiled to himself. And probably spoiled rotten.

Jake had a company of sixty-five Rangers, six teams of men, each with meetings and training and desk work and never enough time. With all the paper work he had, he shouldn't be here today. He should have stayed on post, instead of joining B Company for this unscheduled river patrol. But something was going on in Mexico, he told Colonel Gordon, and there were things they needed to see for themselves.

With what they'd found today here at Lloyd Madison's, he was glad he'd come along. There was a lot more than what it looked like.

Fred, outside on Madison's front porch, stuck his head inside the door and called, "Company coming."

Men's voices and the clatter of hooves sounded in the lane. Buggy wheels rattled to a stop in front of the house.

Jake slipped the little photograph into his shirt pocket, set Ruthie down, and walked over to the window. He pulled the curtain aside.

A male voice shouted, "You inside the house. This is the sheriff talking. Come outside now, and that's an order."

Jake frowned. "Miz Annie, who are all those people?"

"They're from El Paso—the mayor, city councilmen, and the deputy sheriff."

Jake let the curtain drop back and started for the door. Fred met him halfway and walked with him. Together, they stepped out onto the porch, past the sagging door. "Which one of you is the sheriff?" Jake said.

A tall man with a brushy mustache stared hard at Jake. Hand on the butt of his revolver, he said, "I'm Deputy Sheriff Morgan. Who are you and what's your business here?"

"I'm Captain Jake Nelson, and this is Sergeant Fred Barkley. We're Texas Rangers from Camp Annex—"

"I don't see no badges," Sheriff Morgan said.

"Rangers don't wear them."

"You got some identification?"

Jake swore under his breath and felt in his shirt pocket behind Elizabeth's photograph. He pulled out his folded Warrant of Authority, an impressive document all Ranger officers carried with them.

Instead of dismounting, the sheriff stayed on his horse and reached his hand out for the paper. The deputy was outranked and he knew it. So did everyone with him. Jake walked down the steps. With a composed expression he passed the paper up without a word. The sheriff glanced at it, handed it back.

"Now stand down, Sheriff, and let's work together. This house was invaded this morning." Standing by the sheriff's horse, Jake called to the house. "Rangers, show yourselves."

Nine men in shirts and ties and Stetsons, with pistols on both hips, filed out the front door. Last in line was a scowling Cavalry officer carrying a rifle. Stone-faced, they stood stiffly on the porch alongside Fred.

"Lieutenant," the sheriff said to the only man wearing a blue uniform, "I thought you guys didn't like each other."

Lieutenant Taylor stared back. "You thought wrong, Sheriff."

"I guess you're Rangers, all right," the sheriff said to Jake. He blinked at the display of men and firepower and cleared his throat. "You realize I didn't know who you were or why you're here."

Jake gave a curt nod. "Why are *you* here?"

"I'll answer that." Mayor Jackson, a short stocky man on a spotted horse, dismounted and walked toward Jake, his hand outstretched. "Our sincere apologies, Captain. Thank you for coming. We're all on edge today. You say this house was invaded? So was the El Paso courthouse. We were attacked by Mexican troops this afternoon. They shot our sheriff, killed the newspaper editor, Lloyd Madison, and abducted his sister at gunpoint."

Jake winced. The news hit him like a kick in the chest.

Lloyd Madison had been his friend. Now Lloyd was dead and his beautiful sister kidnapped.

A helpless anger welled up inside him.

The warning had come too late.

Four

HER HANDS WERE SHAKING AGAIN. Elizabeth gripped the reins of the little horse they'd put her on and fought another wave of exhaustion. She looked up at the cloudless hot sky and silently prayed for strength again. Over and over during the day she asked Jesus to get her out of this, but so far she'd had no answer or any sign of one.

For the third straight day she'd ridden with the Mexicans across open desert flatland. Like the day before, today was baking hot, the sun burning the air, drying her mouth, making it hard to breathe. The scenery had changed. The flatland was turning hilly now. They went through canyons, squeezed between mountains towering above them.

Here and there, shafts of sunlight wove through the tall pines overhead. She tried to concentrate, to memorize where she was, but the uniforms, the guns, the hard-eyed stares of the soldiers alongside turned her insides to jelly.

She forced herself to be calm. She and Lloyd had decided only that morning to go early to the courthouse. Which meant these men didn't know who she was. And would it help her or hurt her when they found out she was Lloyd's sister and who her father was?

They'd known from the minute they walked in who Lloyd was. And they'd killed him.

The hours dragged, and she would have fallen off the horse twice if the major alongside hadn't watched her. She'd never liked horses. Secretly she was afraid of them.

She'd grown up in a big house with servants. Living in Washington with private carriages and horse-drawn street-cars in town, she had no need to ride a horse. In fact, she knew so little about horses she used to laugh and say she could hardly tell the front end of one from the back end. But three days on horseback with Mexican soldiers, who rode like Indians, proved how little she knew. Her back end ached up to her neck, and both knees throbbed.

The uncertainty of not knowing where they were taking her pressed in on her. She'd thought she was handling it rather well until, with no warning, her hands started to shake uncontrollably.

At first, they expected her to cook. She hurt so much she could hardly stand, and sitting was out of the question. When she told them she didn't know how to cook over a fire, they didn't believe her, shoved a sack of rice at her and pointed to the fire.

The major brought her a pail of water. She blinked at him. When he shrugged, she dumped the sack of rice into the water and hung it over the fire. She lay down on her stomach under a tree to keep an eye on it and fell asleep. Later, clouds of steam rose. Great clouds of steam.

Elizabeth lay curled up under a tree, her eyes closed.

∽

For the third time in as many minutes, Captain Jake Nelson raised the field glasses to his eyes.

"She shouldn't do that," he muttered. "Leaves her too vulnerable to the Mexican soldiers."

So far they hadn't really hurt her. They'd jerked her around a couple of times and pushed her, but nothing too serious. Yet.

"How many men, Jake?" Gus asked him.

Jake lowered the glasses. "Still six soldiers and the major. He seems able to control them so far. If they were going to kill her, I think they would have done so by now. Taking her back to Diego—which seems the best guess to where they're going—slows them down." He raised the glasses again and stiffened.

"Uh-oh."

"What's happening?"

"One of them kicked her and woke her up. They look like they're arguing. He just slapped her."

Jake shook his head and gave a dry chuckle with no humor in it. "She has no idea of the danger she's in. She just hauled off and slapped him back. He looks surprised."

He passed the glasses to the other two men. "If they hurt her now, we're too far away to help. Let's get her out of there tonight. Pack up. It'll take us a while to get to her."

∽

Elizabeth jumped up, grabbed a long stick, and stirred the rice. She couldn't stir fast enough. No one could, she thought. Chunky white foam sputtered and frothed, pouring

37

over the rim, coursing down the sides of the bucket like a waterfall. The fire hissed. With a ladle she skimmed off rice into another pot, then another. And another. Nothing helped, and they had no more pots anyway. The pail of rice kept growing and hissing and boiling over. The ground was burning.

The major stomped over. With a disgusted look he threw a pail of water at it.

The fire sputtered out.

Nobody would talk to her.

They ate cold beans and tortillas that night.

At bedtime, wrapped in a blanket, she forced herself to stay awake until the soldiers were asleep. They were all hungry and mad at her. She dreaded nightfall, never knowing when one of them would creep over to her in the middle of the night. So far, orders from the major had kept them away, but she suspected time was growing short in that department.

Today had been especially worrisome. Two of the soldiers watched everything she did, smiling and making hand signals to each other. Not a good sign.

Each night they tied her wrists and ankles so she couldn't escape when they were sleeping. Not very likely, she thought. Seven of them and one of her, but the major had gone off that night. That bothered her. With him gone, they could be anywhere. Once it was dark, she couldn't keep track of where the men were.

She tried to roll over, but with her hands tied behind her back, she was uncomfortable. They were in a small clearing with trees all around, and the night was noisy with crickets and owl hoots. A wolf called in the distance, raising the hair on her arms. Close by, another answered. She shuddered and wriggled deeper under the blanket.

The night weighed heavy on her eyelids. With a shaky sigh she closed her eyes.

Shortly after three o'clock that morning, something warned her awake.

Was it one of the Mexicans or was it the wolf?

Her mouth went dry.

Rigid, she slitted her eyes open. The hairs on the back of her neck lifted as a dark shadow loomed over her.

For a moment she forgot how to breathe.

It was a man with a knife. He was absolutely silent and as black as the night.

He wore all black—shirt, pants, gloves. A black hood covered his head, leaving only an oval of face exposed. Even that was blackened. All she saw were the whites of eyes and teeth. He looked like a skull.

A scream forced up from her chest. A heavy palm clamped her mouth and pinned her head to the ground. Elizabeth, fighting for her life, struggled against his hands, writhing, arching, flailing her tied-together legs. She jerked her head to pull away, but strong fingers gripped her face.

"Don't scream," a voice hissed in her ear.

Mouth wide open under his hand, she heaved her body sideways and felt his thumb pop into her mouth. Elizabeth clamped her teeth on it.

He snatched his thumb out and reared back. "Blast it, woman, you bit me!" a surprised Texas accent growled. Squatting alongside, he hauled her up into a sitting position.

Deep chuckles came from the darkness.

"All right, you two, you think it's so funny, get over here

and help me untie her. Just keep away from her mouth. She's vicious!"

Two other dark forms appeared and went down on their knees beside her. Like him, they also wore black, their faces as black as his. Both of them were grinning.

"Who . . . what are you?" Elizabeth asked, her voice trembling.

The one she bit glared down at her. "I'm Captain Jake Nelson; these two are Sergeant Fred Barkley and Sergeant Gus Dukker. We're Frontier Battalion Rangers. We're taking you home, unless you bite one of us again."

"I'm sorry I bit you. I've never seen anyone painted black like that. I didn't know what you were."

The hard lines in his face didn't soften a bit. "We wear black as a night disguise. It's used by all the military." He rested his hand on her shoulder. "Didn't mean to frighten you. Don't move. I'm going to cut you loose."

The knife at her back slit through the ropes as if they were paper. She tried not to think how sharp it must be.

"How many men here tonight?" he asked.

"Six."

"We counted seven this afternoon."

"The major was here, but he left early. He said he'd be back before daylight."

"Then we got them all. We killed six."

Her eyes widened. "You killed six men? I didn't hear a thing."

A corner of his mouth dug in, a black dent in a black cheek. "You weren't supposed to. When they talked, did they ever mention Diego—General Manuel Diego?"

"Several times. They were to meet him in San Jose."

He swore softly. "I thought so."

He threw her blanket aside. "Good, you're dressed. Let's put a little distance between us and this place. Then, soon as it's light, you'll put on the boys' clothes we brought. Three men and a woman might raise questions. Four men are less likely to."

He stood, pulled her up alongside, then started across the clearing in long strides toward the horses. She broke into a stumbling run to keep up with him, but her feet had been tied together for hours and felt clumsy. Trying to hurry, one foot caught the back of her ankle and pitched her forward. He shot his arms out and grabbed her around the waist, behind the knees.

Without missing a stride, he lifted her against him. "You all right?" He gave off an air of confidence and strength.

She nodded. "I'm sorry." With a tired sigh she leaned her head against him. Under her cheek she felt the bunch and pull of heavy chest muscles. For the first time in three days, she realized, she felt safe.

Which made no sense. These men were Texas Rangers and had just killed six Mexican soldiers without a sound.

Outlaws were terrified of them.

Why wasn't she?

When they'd reached a group of horses and mules, the captain shifted her higher in his arms. "One leg on each side of the saddle," he said, and sat her on a dark horse she recognized as belonging to the Mexicans. He handed her the reins.

She cleared her throat. "I don't ride very well," she said.

"I noticed."

Her chin lifted. "I grew up in Washington and never

had to ride. And if I did, I certainly wouldn't ride like this, straddled across a horse. It's not ladylike."

"No, but it's the only sensible way to ride a horse, male or female. And when we get you in some decent riding clothes, it's going to save your life."

She smiled. "Just when did you notice my riding ability—or the lack thereof?"

"Yesterday afternoon. I watched you through field glasses." As he bent and shortened the stirrups for her legs, she caught a quick flash of white teeth in the dark face.

"You can't cook either," he said.

She narrowed her eyes at him. "I have the distinct feeling you've been spying on me."

He nodded. "For the last two days, Duchess. Be glad we caught up with you so soon." He swung up on the horse next to hers, his face serious. His gaze held hers. "We rode hard to get here. If they're taking you where I think they are, you'd be there tomorrow, and you wouldn't like it."

"Is that why you came in tonight?"

"It's one of the reasons we're going out now, instead of waiting for daylight. The other reason is because we were afraid they'd kill you."

He reached over and covered her hand holding the reins. His hands were half again the size of hers. When she started to ease her hand away, he tightened his fingers around hers. "These mountains are high with dangerous drop-offs. I'll lead you down. Gus, you go ahead, nice and slow. Fred, you follow us with the pack mule."

He made a small clicking sound with his teeth and started down the mountainside.

For an hour they moved downhill quietly, following a

path on the far side of the clearing to avoid Major Chavez on his return.

They wound down a trail bordered by high, dark cliffs on one side, a forty-foot fall of empty air on the other. He let his horse choose the way, the hoofbeats muffled by layers of pine needles and spongy moss.

Night pressed in, a breathing, silent blackness. For the first time since she was a little girl, she felt afraid of the dark. She tried to force the fear away, but it lay like ice in the pit of her stomach. She could see nothing, not even the man alongside her.

The sky was black.

The trail was black.

Where did one end, the other begin?

"How can the horses see where they're going?" To her dismay, her voice wobbled.

"To a horse, it's dusk, not dark," he said. "Trust him. They see better at night than we do."

When her horse grunted and blew his lips, Jake took his hand away and patted the animal's neck, soothing him. "He's a Mexican horse and knows he's got an inexperienced rider on his back. That makes him nervous. He's young and he's smart, just doesn't have enough self-confidence yet."

"And I suppose your horse is different?"

He glanced over at her. "Banjo—that's his name—has so much confidence, he tries to tell *me* what to do."

She shrugged. Why not? A bossy horse for a bossy Ranger.

When he reached a black-gloved hand over and covered hers again, she let out a quiet sigh of relief. She definitely felt safer with him guiding the reins. She looked over at the big dark shape on the horse beside hers and wondered again why she wasn't afraid of him.

∽

Sunrise in the Sierra Madre and the eastern horizon glowed like a line of red-hot coals. In the valley below, pinks and corals streaked the purple sky. Sitting on a hillside, Jake leaned back against a tree and crossed his arms behind his head, drinking in the beauty. This was his favorite part of the day. When he was a boy, he and his mother used to go outside and watch the sunrise. She always said God wrote the gospel not only in the Bible but on trees and flowers and clouds and stars. They used to read the Bible together and discuss it.

He still missed her. Not a day went by he didn't think of her.

God rest her soul.

She'd been gone five years, taken by influenza while he was fighting Apaches in Arizona. He'd wanted so much to get back to her before she died, but he was too far away.

For years she'd been the shield between him and his stepfather, squeezing herself between the two of them and bumping them apart with her hip. It used to be her son she protected from her husband's raging temper, but at fourteen, Jake was filling out. Summers, he worked a full day roping and breaking horses for a nearby rancher. At fifteen he was taller and stronger than his father, and he was still growing.

Her warning changed to "Jake, don't hurt him" the day she came out and found Jake had her husband pinned against the side of the house. One of Jake's eyes was bruised and swollen shut, and blood trickled from his mouth. His fist was balled.

He'd never yet hit his father back, but those days might be over. Jake unclenched his fist at her words and walked away. As he did, his stepfather grabbed up a piece of wood and hit him across the back. Jake knew then he'd have to leave. If he stayed, he was afraid he'd kill the man. His mother would lose a husband and then have to watch her only son hanged for murder.

He loved her too much for that.

Jake was gone the next morning. And so was her Bible.

∞

Gus urged his horse off the trail, to a spring bubbling around a pile of rocks. As his horse drank, Gus looked back at Jake. "We're almost out of the mountains. Where do you want to stop?"

"This will do fine," Jake said. "We need to wash this stuff off and change clothes. Can't chance running into someone else. It'll be commented on."

He swung off his horse, led him to the spring to drink, and handed the reins to Gus. "Let's all of us get cleaned up. You and Fred take care of the horses, fill the canteens, get us ready to go. I'll get the duchess into some other clothes so she looks like a man, and then let's get out of here fast. The sun's coming up. It'll be daylight soon. I know Mexicans, and I won't feel safe until this place is miles behind us."

Elizabeth stiffened. "But I thought we *were* safe now."

"Far from it. When the major returns and finds his men dead and you gone, we'll be the objects of one big Ranger manhunt."

"How would they know Rangers did it?" she asked.

He shrugged. "If you were Texas, who else would you send?"

She thought about that a minute. "There isn't anyone, I guess."

In the half-light of dawn, she resembled her photograph: small face and nose, perfect mouth. What was going through her mind? he wondered. She was no bigger than a minute, but she wasn't cowed. Her hands were folded, clasped in front of her like a nun, giving her an almost serene appearance. But that, he suspected, was for his benefit. Dead-white, the knuckles on her fingers gave her away. She was proud, and if she was afraid, she was hiding it. He'd always liked a woman with a little spunk. She had that all right. She also had—he searched for the word—*class*.

Ruthie's little voice echoed in his mind. *Boo-ful*. Indeed she was. Beautiful and intelligent, both qualities he prized in a woman.

Elizabeth turned in the saddle, as if undecided how to swing her leg over.

"Let's get you down from there." Jake hid a smile. "There is no ladylike way to get off a horse wearing a dress. So lift your right knee over the saddle horn as if you were sitting sidesaddle, then slide down the horse. I'll catch you."

Facing him, she got her leg over the pommel, turned in the saddle, and reached for him.

As she did, an early ray of sun filtered through the branches overhead and highlighted her hands. A flake of sunlight caught itself in the plain gold wedding band and glittered a thousand sparks into his eyes.

His breath caught.

She's married.

Briefly he closed his eyes and wondered how he'd missed it, why he hadn't noticed the ring before. Usually it was the first thing he looked for. He hadn't looked that night because it had been too dark to see.

Her husband, whoever he was, had lucked out because one thing Jake Nelson didn't do was fool around with another man's wife or girlfriend. He'd been down that road before.

A muscle ticked in his cheek.

And now, ten years later, fate was giving him a chance to even the score.

No thanks.

She was married, and married women were off-limits.

When her arms went around his neck, Jake closed his hands around a small, soft waist and pulled her against him.

In that instant, all his good intentions about keeping his hands off married women rose and scattered like a flock of pigeons.

Shaken by how quickly the thought jumped into his mind, he ordered it back.

He heard a quick, sharp intake of breath as he slid her down the length of him. Her startled gaze shot up and locked with his. The pulse throbbing at the base of her throat was tripping like a baby bird's.

His arms, his chest, his legs tingled everywhere she'd touched him. He eased his breath out slowly, aware of his own racing pulse. Somewhere off in the back of his mind, a small alarm bell pinged, reminding him.

She's married.

As soon as her feet touched ground, he dropped his arms and stepped back.

Puzzled by his reaction to her, he went to his horse and dug into the saddlebag for the package of clothes the quarter-master at Fort Bliss had put together for her. He handed the package to her and jerked his head at an overgrown creosote bush a few feet away. He wrinkled his nose. Its pungent tar smell hung heavy in the air, but it was tall and bushy and its waxy green leaves would give her the privacy she needed.

"You can change behind that hedge over there." With an effort, he managed to keep his voice steady, not allowing the shakiness he felt to slip into it.

Fred and Gus were already cleaning themselves up. He turned his back on her and strode over to the pack mule and pulled out a towel and a big piece of soap. He squirmed inside, guessing what he must look like with his face streaked with grease and soot. And he stank so bad of gunpowder and sweat he could smell himself.

He shrugged. So what?

Over the icy little spring he managed to get most of the grease and soot off his face and hands. He sank down, leaned against a tree, and cocked a leg up. For nearly five minutes he knifed the mud from his boots, telling himself it wasn't good for the leather. But he couldn't explain combing his hair and running a razor over his face. What had happened with her back there was a warning to jerk his emotions in line.

He looked back at the creosote bush and rolled his shoulders, forcing them to loosen up. His mind turned.

Something didn't add up, something he couldn't put his finger on. Married or not, she'd felt the same jolt of attraction that had shot through him. He hadn't imagined it, and he hadn't imagined her reaction, either. She'd been as rattled by it as he was.

But he also saw caution in her eyes. Perhaps even a tinge of fear. If she was attracted to him, she didn't want to be. He sucked in a slow breath.

Feeling's mutual, honey. I don't want to be attracted to you, either.

Eyes closed, he forced himself to relax. He drew a couple of deep breaths and focused on those places within himself he needed to change and concentrated. One place demanded immediate attention—a little itchy spot in his mind that Elizabeth had dug herself into and interrupted his thoughts.

A few minutes later, he was quiet inside and felt himself back in control. He'd locked her into a little box in the back of his mind.

"Captain," she called, "my fingers hurt. They don't work right. I managed to undo only three buttons in all this time."

Softly he let loose a cussword. He looked over at Fred. "Her wrists were tied too tight for too long."

"You stay put," Fred said. "You've done most of the work with her. I'll take her dress off."

"No, you won't." Jake jumped to his feet and hurried off toward the bush.

Fred snickered. "She's getting to him."

"And he doesn't even know it," Gus said.

"I figured something was going on after she bit him and all he did was carry her like a little queen to her horse." Fred laughed. "Anybody else would be dead by now."

Five

Elizabeth closed her eyes in a long, slow blink when a tall man with curly blond hair appeared from behind the creosote bush. For a moment she had a sense of tilting reality, of time running backward, of something half remembered. It was as if she were looking at Carl again.

His own gaze was jumping all over her face as if he felt it, too.

"Let's get started on those buttons," Jake said.

Elizabeth stared up at him, and for a minute it was hard to breathe.

Last night it had been so dark and his face so black and scary, nothing about him had registered. In the early morning light and the confusion of getting off the horses, she still hadn't noticed him much. All those dark faces looked the same to her. With Jake, because he was closest to her, she'd received only a fleeting impression of cheekbones, a face full of angles and shadows, and a mouth that could've been carved in stone, all hidden under a layer of soot.

Now, however, he'd managed to get all the soot and disguise washed off. The faint scent of soap and male sweat assaulted her. He was bigger than Carl, but their hair and eyebrows were the same pale blond.

Like Lieutenant Carl Evans, Jake Nelson was a towhead, his hair just as light and thick and touching the back of his collar. But there the resemblance stopped. He looked to be in his late twenties, older than Carl, inches taller and pounds heavier, and his eyes were gray, not brown, like Carl's.

For some reason he looked harder than Carl. Two very different men. Yet every time she looked at him, she had a strange sense of having walked this way before.

She lowered her eyes, unsettled by a tug of attraction to this big slow-talking man. The wrong man.

Elizabeth stiffened her shoulders, reached into the back of her mind, and switched the memories off. After three years, she was getting pretty good at that, at turning off what she didn't want to remember.

She glanced at Jake uneasily. *He's a Texas Ranger.*

Carl had called Rangers—criticized them, really—as being shock troops. Their initial response to an Indian attack was overwhelming firepower delivered at full gallop. Speed, surprise, violence—an "annihilation charge," they called it.

And she bit him.

She didn't know whether to burst out laughing or get up and run.

Firmly she cleared the huskiness from her voice. "Where are you from, Captain?"

"Up near Oklahoma, little town called Burkburnett."

His cheeks puffed the *b*'s, his words leaning lazily on each other. Typical Texas twang, she thought.

She straightened her shoulders and wrestled the corners of her mouth into a smile.

Be nice. Talk to the man.

She held her hands out and waggled her fingers. "They're like sticks. They don't bend right." She swallowed and looked up. "I'm sorry to ask you. I know you don't want to do this."

His hand closed around her wrist and led her into the sunlight streaming through the branches, where he could see the green dress better. Frowning, he pinched a tiny button in his fingers and gave a soft snort through his nose.

"No wonder you can't unbutton them. They're like baby teeth!" He pinched and pulled. A piece of green thread and a white button dangled from his fingers.

He rubbed his nose back and forth. "Looks like I broke it."

Lips pursed, Elizabeth looked down at her front and the fifteen other tiny buttons that went down to her waist. "This isn't going to work, Captain. We'll be here all day. Your fingers are like sausages."

"Thanks for the compliment, but if we want to stay alive, we haven't got all day. So stand still and stop your yapping." He stooped on the balls of his feet in front of her, his eyes narrowed, intense, looking almost silver in the light.

Evidently this determined man did exactly what he put his mind to. And if she didn't like it, too bad.

In ten minutes he had her unbuttoned and holding her arms up while he lifted the green silk dress over her head. Then he removed the two petticoats. Finally, heat sliding down her neck, she stood before him, bare-armed, in her chemise and pantaloons.

She was uncomfortable and embarrassed and angry at herself for being either. She looked up at him helplessly and started to giggle. "I am mortified. Don't you say a word. Not one word, you hear?"

He smiled. "I've seen ladies in pantaloons before."

"Oh, of course. You're married?"

"No."

"Sorry, Captain, I shouldn't have asked."

"My name's Jake." He glanced up at her. "How long have you been married?"

"I'm a widow. My husband was Carl Evans, a lieutenant in the Seventh Cavalry. He was killed in a Comanche raid three years ago." She looked away.

"I surely am sorry to hear that." His face was serious, his voice gentle. "I assumed you were married when I saw the ring."

"Wearing it eliminates a lot of questions, especially when traveling alone. A wedding ring keeps unwanted contacts away. Most men leave a married woman alone."

He held open the brown denim pants and a soft red flannel shirt he'd brought her from Fort Bliss.

"Come on, Lizzy, let's put your britches on." He cocked his head at her. "Anyone ever call you that?"

"No," she said, and burst out laughing. She stepped into the trousers and shrugged on the shirt, watching while he pulled the waistband out and stuffed the shirttail in all around.

Soon she was dressed, her feet laced into riding boots two sizes too big. Quickly she pulled her hair back, braided it into a loose pigtail, and he stuffed it up under a cowboy hat.

"Thank you," she said. "Though you won't admit it, underneath all that gruff officer persona, I suspect you're rather sweet."

He gave a short bark of a laugh. "Lady, I've been called a lot of things by a lot of women, but *sweet* sure wasn't one of them."

He tweaked her Stetson. "Come on, pretty boy, let's ride."

Half an hour later, they were back on the Chihuahuan desert. She recognized it now, miles and miles of parched land, a dry desert basin lying between mountain ranges. The rhythmic thud of horses' hooves still kicked up clouds of red dirt, but high overhead on the rimrock, something new had been added. Noisy green parrots swept from tree to tree, scolding them. Ponds appeared here and there in the landscape, and butterflies were everywhere.

The horses clattered across a plank bridge over a creek and followed a twisty back trail through the trees. Twice they saw small settlements in the distance and detoured well out past them.

Before they'd left the little spring, Jake had tied her to the saddle so she couldn't fall out when they rode fast. Like now.

He looked over. "Watch me and do what I do." He kicked his horse into a canter.

Elizabeth imitated him. Lightly she slapped the reins and kicked her horse, startled when the animal broke into a sedate little rolling gallop. She threw a triumphant look at Jake and grinned. He looked as surprised as she was and pleased at what she'd done.

"Starting to get the hang of this, are you?" he said.

"And about time, you're thinking."

"Not at all. You catch on fast."

She wasn't so sure.

These three men, sitting relaxed and loose in their saddles, could ride for days. She tightened her knees into the horse and felt the tension ease across her shoulders. She had to admit, riding in trousers made far more sense than riding in a dress.

In late afternoon he pointed out their objective—a line of mountain peaks shimmering in the heat way off in the distance but slowly, slowly coming closer. She didn't much like the idea of going back up into mountains, but Jake insisted it was better than sleeping out in the rain. This section of Chihuahua's Sierra Madre, he said, was honeycombed with caves.

He knew of a cavern deep inside one of the mountains where they could keep dry, have a cook fire, and get a good night's sleep.

"We're all tired," he said.

That sounded wonderful, especially since it had started to rain an hour before and, by now, she was soaked. She looked up at the lead-colored sky and wiped the wetness off her cheek. "I didn't know it ever rained in a desert."

"Depends when and where it is. It's the August monsoon season, and the high Texas and Mexican deserts see rain every year about this time."

Fred smiled over at her. "Rain is good. If anyone tries to follow us tonight, they're out of luck. Rain like this wipes out horse tracks."

As the sun began to set, they cut out of the desert and onto a rocky trail that wound up the mountainside. Trees, sparse at first, grew thicker as they climbed, and then they crowded in so close that she could reach out and touch them. She raised her eyes overhead. Here and there, small patches of daylight filtered through the canopy of leaves. They climbed higher. When Jake pointed out a shiny cliffside and said it was the entrance to the cave, she shook her head.

"I see nothing but wet rock," she said.

"Good. If you can't see it, neither will the Mexicans."

Night in the Sierra Madre drew in swiftly. As soon as the sun slipped behind the mountain peaks, cold shadows swept down the slopes and blanketed the valleys in rainy darkness.

Hidden by thick bushes, a large black opening appeared in the rock. Hunched low over their horses, they entered single-file. A few feet away from the entrance, darkness fell like a curtain behind them. Not a trace of light got through.

The men dismounted and unloaded the big mule of the supplies they'd taken from the Mexicans. Each came back with a lantern, which they lit quickly. They needed plenty of light to lead the horses and mule well back into the cave.

There, the animals would be protected from the rain and any horse odors would be contained inside.

"Only an Indian can track at night," Jake said. "An Indian scout can smell horse manure a mile away. We're taking no chances."

Once off her horse, Elizabeth stood in the circle of lantern light, surprised at how large the cavern was. The ceiling—if there was one—disappeared into blackness overhead. Hesitating, she reached a hand out to the smooth stone wall. It was damp and cold. Air currents stirred above, a whisper of wind from the entrance. From somewhere came the sound of dripping water.

"This place is creepy," she said.

Fred went out to find firewood and kindling to start a cook fire. He found a pile of damp mesquite blown back under a ledge by the wind and partially protected from the rain. "Once we get a fire going, it'll dry out just fine."

The Rangers had stripped the Mexicans' food supplies and now had flour, sugar, coffee—things they'd done without on their rush down from Texas.

∞

Supper that night was quail that Gus and Fred had shot earlier in the afternoon. They roasted the little birds on a primitive spit over the fragrant mesquite. Elizabeth was astounded by how much these men knew about cooking. Beans and hot biscuits rounded out their dinner.

Smiling, she sat with her quail in her lap, fingers flying, picking every shred of meat off the tiny bones. "I hadn't realized how hungry I was. What a relief to eat with people who aren't planning to kill you."

Afterward, she warmed herself near the smoldering embers of the fire. "When will we get back to Texas? Day after tomorrow?"

Fred shot a look at Gus and then shoved to his feet. He stuck out his hand and pulled Gus up. "How 'bout we go spread out the blankets and unroll the bed sacks?"

∞

Jake had wondered when she'd get around to asking that. He waited until Gus and Fred and their lantern glow disappeared around a corner, then said, "I wish we could go back right away, but that's not likely to happen. With any luck, we may be able to go back next week."

She stiffened. "Next week? Why next week? I need to go home now. I've got a little niece with no family and I'm frantic about her."

"Right now, I expect Ruthie is safer than she'll ever be

in her life again. I took her to Fort Bliss with me when we left your house. At your father's request, she's staying with Colonel Gordon and his family until he gets there. She has other children to play with and a twenty-four-hour guard."

"Guard? You think she's still in danger?"

"I'm not sure. Your housekeeper told one of my men that the Mexicans wanted to take her with them, but the major overruled it." He threw another piece of wood on the fire. Damp, it smoked for a minute, then popped and sent a burst of sparks flying upward. "A revolt against President Hector Guevara is brewing in Mexico."

"I know. Lloyd recognized Major Chavez in the courthouse. He said Diego is the brains behind the revolt."

"He's probably right, but the U.S. needs that confirmed absolutely. That's what Fred and Gus and I hope we can find out. Nobody wants another war with Mexico."

"So, Gus and Fred are in on this as well?"

Jake nodded. "We're all part of an operation." He sighed and stood up. "I'm going to leave you with friends of mine about twenty miles from here. You'll like his wife. She's half Aztec and teaches English at a monastery. They're good people."

"Which is why you chose this cave," she said.

"And why—for your own safety and theirs—I didn't tell you before."

He also didn't tell her that his friend was a former Ranger he'd served with. He and Ricardo Romero had saved each other's lives several times. Jake considered Ricardo the brother he never had. He saw the Romeros a couple of times a year, on official trips or "unofficial" business, like now.

"You'll be at their house three or four days until I learn if Diego was involved or not. Then I'll come get you and take you home."

Her chin lifted. "And what if something happens to you?"

"My friend knows what to do. He'll take you across the Rio Grande to the nearest Ranger river patrol in Texas. He'll get you to them, and the Rangers will take you to Fort Bliss." His mouth was tight and serious. "Know this: You will be in no more danger with him than with me. I'd trust Ricardo with my life."

He'd taken his hat off and dropped it to one side. In the firelight, the hair falling over his forehead had a reddish cast to it.

White-faced, Elizabeth stood. Lips trembling, she said, "I see. It's all arranged. Why didn't you trust me? I would have helped you any way I could. You see me as a woman with nothing to contribute except needlepoint and children. Well, Captain, I have a degree to go along with my needlework. I am not a silly socialite. I was raised with politics and confidentiality and the consequences of war. Patriotism is not the exclusive domain of males. Like you—and Lloyd—I also love my country. When I get back to Texas, I'm going to run his newspaper."

She turned and walked away from the fire, toward the cave wall where their blankets were spread.

Jake threw his hand out. "Elizabeth, I'm sorry. Wait . . ."

She waved him off without answering. He heard a little choking sound as she disappeared into the darkness.

He pulled in a slow breath. Guilt flashed through his mind. She was about to cry.

Half an hour later, Jake grabbed a lantern and climbed to

his feet. "I'm going to check the horses." Without waiting for a reply, he started for the back of the cave. The lantern's swinging light threw his shadow, huge and dark, onto the cave wall alongside.

∽

Gus reached into his jacket and pulled out a flask of whiskey. "How many times he gonna check? That's the third time he went down there."

Fred held out his cup so Gus could pour drinks for them both. "It's not the horses he's checking, you know. He passes the bed sacks on the way." Gus sighed. "I hate to see him look like that. He's miserable. Did you see the look on his face the first time he came back and said she was crying?"

"Yeah." Fred picked up Jake's empty cup. "Pour some of that in here to take his mind off her."

Gus snorted quietly. "He won't touch it. His old man was a drunk. Told me he left home at fifteen to get away from him. In all the years I've known Jake, I've never seen him take a drink."

"Then hide it in his coffee," Fred said. "He needs something tonight. And do it now—he's coming back. I see his lantern."

"Gotcha. Give me his cup."

∽

A few moments later, Gus asked, "Horses all right, Jake?"
"Yeah, they're fine."
"How's our duchess doing? Still crying?"
"Yeah."

"She'll be all right tomorrow. Come on over here and have some coffee."

Jake took the coffee and then sat and leaned his back against the cave wall. Staring at the fire, he sipped it and said, "Coffee tastes different—what is it?"

"Some of that Mexican coffee. Got it from their supplies. You like it?"

"Dunno. It's kind of spicy." But it wasn't long before he'd drained the cup. He held it out for a refill. "You really think she'll be all right tomorrow?"

Gus took the cup and turned around to the coffeepot and his flask, his back to Jake. "Sure. Women are like that. Get all stirred up about the littlest of things, and then it's all over and they get on with their lives. While us poor guys stew for days."

Fred pulled out a deck of cards. "How about a couple hands to take your mind off things?"

Elizabeth's angry blue eyes floated across his mind, eyes fighting back tears.

"I'm in," Jake said. Five minutes later, so was Elizabeth—still in his mind, settled in for the night apparently. He stared at his cards, trying to forget her.

She wasn't his type, anyway. She was a senator's daughter and spoiled rotten. He knew that the first time he saw her picture. Grimly he set his teeth together. Everything he did with her, he did all wrong. He'd become short-tempered, disorganized, and more than a little rough around the edges because he knew she didn't like it. And yet he found one excuse after another to hang around her. It made no sense.

He dragged a hand down his face.

And if she hates you now, just wait till she finds out about you and her brother.

She was smart, he'd give her that. He always did like smart women. His mother taught him that. She was a schoolteacher in Greensburg, outside San Antonio. Too smart to have married Harvey, his stepfather, but she'd married him anyway.

Pregnant with Jake, his mother had wanted a name for her unborn child. She wanted better for her baby, even if it meant a poor marriage for herself. Jake's real father, a Deputy U.S. Marshal, had been killed two weeks before their wedding—shot in the back by a convicted bank robber.

A rush of sympathy tore through Jake for a towheaded little boy with hair in his eyes whose stepfather hated him. Every time he climbed onto his lap, Harvey set him down firmly on the floor, saying, "Stay offa me, kid."

And Jake had cried.

His throat tightened now, remembering. He shook his head and forced the gloom away. This wasn't like him at all. He frowned at his coffee.

The three men played cards for an hour, the other two laughing, having a good time. Normally a good player, Jake lost one hand after another. Time and again, someone re-filled his coffee cup. Though he said little, he was glad they were there. Like most military men, he liked the bonding and camaraderie of fellow soldiers. Gus and Fred were ex-cavalry, too. Rangers, especially, looked after each other in ways other men never did. With another Ranger, you always knew where you stood.

Men were predictable.

Sometime around midnight, when he fanned his cards,

Jake realized he couldn't tell a club from a spade. Head whirling, he tossed them down. "Count me out. I'm so tired, I can't see straight."

He struggled to his feet and went weaving off into the darkness. Twice he stumbled. It took concentration just to place one foot in front of the other. Then he tripped and found himself on his knees on the cave floor. In the dim glow of a lantern, the bed sacks and blankets were just ahead.

It was too much effort to get up. He crawled the last few feet to the bed sacks and pitched forward onto the first one he came to.

"Wrong bed, Captain," a high, sharp voice cut through the dark.

"You 'sleep, 'Lizabeth?"

"Not anymore."

"What's wrong?"

"Not a thing."

"You're still mad because I didn't tell you." He rolled onto his back and threw an arm out. "Oops. What are you doing here?"

Elizabeth shoved the heavy arm off her midsection and sat up. "This is my bed, not yours." She turned her face away. "Phew, you're drunk."

"Am I?" He blew out a long sigh. "You may be right."

"Go to your own bed. Now!"

"I'm going, I'm going. Where is it?"

He tried to push himself up and sprawled onto his face instead. His nose flattened against the blanket. The world lurched into a slow spin. He winced and closed his eyes to stop the whirling.

In seconds, he was asleep.

∞

Shortly before Elizabeth woke up the next morning, Jake went outside and stuck his head in a bucket of cold water, but it didn't help. He'd had only a few hours' sleep and it showed in the lines of his face. Weary, he rubbed his face with both hands and returned to the cave to finish getting dressed.

The dull, throbbing headache that had woken him that morning was thumping his ears like a bass drum, and his mouth tasted like old socks. Worse, he'd made a fool of himself last night, collapsing onto Elizabeth's bed sack.

A hangover—another first. A little fumble-fingered, he handed her a clean shirt and trousers, turned his back and waited while she put them on. Then he moved to help her with the buttons.

"I'll button myself," she said, and pushed his hands away.

"You can't, so slide your hand under the buttons and stand still."

Quickly he buttoned her up and laced her boots, all while trying to figure out how and why last night had happened the way it did. He'd never been drawn to any girl this fast, and he intended to stop it cold. Right now. He had no time for women in his life.

When he finished, he stepped back and looked at her. "Thank you for not mentioning last night. I'm sorry about it. Charge it off to foolish friends who slipped liquor into my coffee. I don't drink. It never happened before, and it never will again."

Six

JAKE GUIDED BANJO DOWN through a mixed forest of pines and towering oak trees covering the mountainside. He reined to a stop and pointed to a large farmhouse below, overlooking a sweeping bend of the Rio Verde in the distance. "That's their house," he said.

Built of whitewashed adobe, the house had wooden shutters and painted beams. Pots of geraniums soaking up the sun on a second-floor balcony added a bright Mexican touch. Two barns and several corrals lay beyond.

Jake waved to a dark-haired man running from the house. When the man came closer, Jake and Fred both jumped off their horses and rushed forward to greet him. The three of them laughed and hugged and thumped each other's backs.

Elizabeth watched. This was more than casual friends meeting. Since Fred and Jake were both Rangers, Ricardo must be, too. For some reason, that did not make her feel any better.

"Jake! Jake!" A woman carrying a little girl hurried down the hill toward them. Behind her, two young boys slammed out of the house and ran to catch up. The toddler in her arms squealed and waved at Jake.

Smiling, Jake strode to meet them, kissed the woman on both cheeks and took the girl from her.

He kissed her and swung her around until she was giggling. Then he set her down and turned to the boys, who rushed up and hugged him.

He spoke to the mother in a guttural language Elizabeth didn't understand. Aztec. Ricardo's wife was half Indian.

Switching to English, Jake introduced Elizabeth to Maria and Ricardo Romero and their two boys.

The little girl turned shy and wrapped both arms around Jake's leg. Hugging his thigh, she looked at Elizabeth and grinned.

Jake laughed and ruffled the child's hair. "And this proper young lady is Jakina. She'll be three next month." He handed her to her mother and looked at his friends, his expression turning serious. "Ricardo, Maria, I need your help." The three of them stepped aside to talk.

A few minutes later, Elizabeth nodded when Ricardo turned to her with a little bow. "Señora Evans, we are honored to have you in our home. You and Fred Barkley—another old friend—are most welcome."

She looked at Ricardo with a half smile. "You Rangers do stick together, don't you?"

He laughed. "As they say, like glue."

Jake took her shoulders and turned her to face him. "Smarty, you figured that out fast. Hey, don't look so worried," he added.

Elizabeth grabbed both of his hands and held them tight. Looking up at him, she whispered, "Please don't leave me here. Take me with you. I'll help any way I can, and I won't be any trouble, I promise."

"Taking you with me would be dangerous and might get us both killed. You're safer here with Fred and Ricardo than with me." He pulled his hands free and traced a finger lightly down her cheek.

Her breath caught. He'd never touched her before unless it was absolutely necessary.

"Stay here, eat good food, and get yourself some rest. I'll see you in a few days. Good-bye, Duchess."

She blinked at him, surprised. She'd been wrong. Until that minute, she'd thought he called her that only when he was angry. His face had a masked, unreadable expression, one she'd seen earlier.

"I have to go now," he said. He stepped into the stirrup and swung himself up easily into the saddle. Touching his heels to Banjo, he started back up the hillside.

When he reached the tree line, he swung around and waved his hat at her. The sunlight slanting through the trees caught in his straw-colored hair and turned it almost golden.

She swallowed past the tightness in her throat. Tough as he was, Jake Nelson was all she had right now. In the past couple of days he'd saved her life, cooked her food, and even helped to dress her. And he'd made it all seem so commonplace and natural, nothing to be embarrassed about.

When she looked embarrassed, he'd made some silly remark or joke which got her laughing.

She owed him for all that.

"Please watch over him, Lord," she whispered as he disappeared into the trees.

Not wanting to be seen together, the Rangers had separated that morning. Gus had split off and taken one of the main trails leading to San Jose, a small farming community ten miles deeper into Mexico. Jake would meet him there later that afternoon. And Fred would stay with her at the Romeros'.

Maria Romero touched her arm and nodded toward the house. "Don't look so worried. Jake will be all right."

Elizabeth looked away quickly. "I'm sure he will."

"That man is good at what he does."

Elizabeth gave a small huff. Which is *what* exactly? she wondered.

Maria picked up the saddlebag of Elizabeth's clothes and led her into the house and upstairs to a room off a long hall overlooking the kitchen. The room contained a small dresser and a single bed. A colorful patchwork quilt lay folded over the footboard. A white lace curtain covered a small window.

Maria set the saddlebag on the bed. "Now, let's get you out of those boy's clothes. I'll bring you up some things of mine. After that long ride, Jake thought you might like a hot bath. The tub is next door, and the boys are filling it now."

∞

It was an old-fashioned metal tub. Elizabeth removed her clothes and let them fall to the floor. They smelled like horse.

She wrinkled her nose. Ugh, *she* smelled like horse.

She stepped into the tub and slid into the hot water. Head back, eyes closed, she luxuriated in it. The heat relaxed her. She stuck her head underwater to wet her hair, then lathered up the bar of soap and rubbed until her scalp felt clean and fluffy suds lay on the water. She dunked her head under again to rinse it and came up smiling.

Thoughts of Jake and Fred and Gus and their brave decision to come after her flew at her from all directions. Texans saving another Texan.

With no warning, her face crumpled. She hiccupped on a sob, and hot tears blended with the water on her face. She was so grateful to them. Mouth twisting, she wept quietly. She hadn't realized how terrified she'd been.

She wrung her hair out and winced. A dull headache, made worse by the tears, throbbed behind her eyes.

After she climbed out, she flexed her fingers. They moved easily. Jake was right. He'd said nothing looked broken.

A slight annoyance at him welled up. The man had dumped her on top of a mountain with complete strangers. She didn't even know where she was!

She watched herself drying off in a mirror. She was in his friend's house, bathing in a tub he'd probably used in the past. She looked at the towel and wondered if he'd ever used it. Somehow, it all felt right.

Wrong.

Despite that masculine Texas courtesy with women, he was a Texas Ranger, part of the Frontier Battalion which, although not U.S. Army, was just as military. She didn't need that complicating her life again. She pulled on the clean chemise and the blue housedress Maria had left on the bed and went down to the kitchen.

Sausages and scrambled eggs steamed in a plate on the table. Elizabeth's stomach rumbled, and she sat down to the first normal meal in a week.

The kitchen was huge. Lacy ferns spilled from pots on a windowsill. In one corner, next to a fireplace, was a counter inset with a firebox and grates for cooking.

Sipping her second cup of coffee, Elizabeth watched as Maria tidied up the kitchen.

"How well do you know our Jake?" Maria asked.

Elizabeth hedged, wondering what Jake had told Ricardo outside about her and what she should say. These people were his friends.

"I hardly know him at all. I didn't meet him until a few days ago, after I was kidnapped and they sent him to get me."

"Nobody sent him. He sent himself."

"What do you mean?"

Maria chuckled. "The story I heard was, when you were taken last week, he went into Colonel Gordon's office and said he was going to Mexico to bring you back. He didn't ask permission to go because crossing into Mexico is a violation of international law, and Colonel Gordon couldn't give it. Jake had planned to go alone, but U.S. Army Intelligence got wind of it and insisted he take two more Rangers with him. Seems both Austin and Washington want to know if Diego had a hand in killing your brother."

Which was what Jake had told her, Elizabeth thought. She drew a deep breath of relief. He hadn't lied to her. For some reason, that was important. The last of the tension drained away.

She'd been with only men for a solid week, and it felt good to talk with another woman. They chatted about everything, including the Texas Rangers.

"Who are a different species altogether, I'm beginning to suspect," Elizabeth said. "I'm not even sure they're human."

Maria chuckled. "I notice you didn't smile when you said that. He's getting to you, eh? Well, he's not as tough as he seems."

Elizabeth's eyebrows went up. "I don't know. He seems pretty tough to me."

"Until you get to know him. Growing up, he didn't have

much of a family. He loved his mother dearly but hated his stepfather, who drank and beat her. And then he beat Jake for trying to stop him."

Elizabeth nibbled on her lower lip. "He's never let on."

Maria nodded. "He probably never will. He's private about a lot of things. At fifteen he left home and joined the Army. At the time, the Army was desperate for new leaders, young men with manners and muscles. They grabbed him on the spot and sent him to specialty schools. At seventeen they made him a second lieutenant. Mind you, they thought he was three years older than he was."

"That's so sad," Elizabeth said. "I had no idea. . . ."

Maria went on, "He also speaks Spanish, French, and Nahuatl, the language of my Aztec ancestors. It's an asset to anyone who works in Mexico, particularly men like Ricardo and Jake. Your brother was also learning it."

A small red flag shot up in Elizabeth's mind. "You know my brother?"

Maria smiled. "You look a lot like him. Must be those bright blue eyes you both have. Jake brought him down to meet Ricardo a couple of months ago."

Elizabeth's breath caught in her throat.

Ricardo Romero was Lloyd's connection in Mexico.

And it got him killed.

∽

"Hey, inside, you ladies decent?" a male voice called.

"Yes, she is," Maria said, laughing. She looked at Elizabeth. "I knew he'd be back."

Jake and the two boys came into the kitchen. At his side, thumb in her mouth, Jakina held his hand.

"I didn't hear you ride in," Elizabeth said. "You forget something?"

He nodded. "Need to find out from Ricardo where the nearest telegraph office is to where I'm going. Last time I was in San Jose they had one, but they might've moved it. I don't want to be asking around where it is. It could raise questions."

Jakina removed her thumb and patted him to get his attention. He stooped and she whispered in his ear. Smiling, he turned her shoulders and gave her a nudge in Elizabeth's direction.

Jakina walked to Elizabeth and peered up at her. She turned to Jake and nodded. "Uncle Jake says you're boo-ful."

Elizabeth raised her eyebrows at Jake. "You said that? That's so nice."

"Ruthie's description of her aunt Elizabeth," he said smoothly. "Run along, kids. Go play and let the grown-ups talk."

Both boys headed for the door. Jakina gave Jake a quick hug and ran after them. The door slammed behind them.

"Those kids do anything he asks," Maria said. "He'll make a wonderful daddy someday."

"Then he better hurry up and get married if he wants a family. In his line of work, his life expectancy isn't the greatest," Elizabeth said.

"Hear that, Maria? Did she just propose to me, or did I hear wrong?"

Maria looked up, grinning. "Heard wrong, I think. By the way, what's this story I hear about you sleeping in her bed last night?"

Elizabeth stiffened. "Oh, for heaven's sake. Don't believe

it, Maria. Your friend fell into my bed sack because he was too drunk to stand up."

Maria looked genuinely surprised. "What? When did you start drinking, Jake?"

"Right after she bit me," he said.

"After she what?" Maria snapped a glance at Elizabeth. "Did you really bite him?"

Elizabeth dropped her face in her hands and blew out a sigh. "It's a long story."

Jake started for the door. Once there, he stopped and turned around. "It's mostly true. Gus and Fred loaded my coffee with whiskey, so I *was* drunk. They're all having a great time with that at my expense. Nothing happened. She was out of that bed sack like a lightning bolt."

He pushed the door open and jerked his head toward the yard. "Come on, Duchess. Let's take a walk."

Seven

ELIZABETH STOOD ON A FLAT GRAY ROCK jutting out from the riverbank and gazed at the tranquil scene before her.

The shallow Rio Verde, dull pea green in the sunlight, moved lazily in the gorge between two mountains. The pine trees crowded on the surrounding hillsides grew straight and tall.

"It's so pretty," she said.

Jake sat on the bank, legs outstretched. "This may be gone by this time next year. Where we're standing could all be underwater. The river's low now, the water controlled by the small irrigation dams upstream."

She noted the edge in his voice and turned to face him. For the first time, his face was tense, his eyes stormy. Surprising for a man who was usually so calm and in control.

Jake pointed up the river toward the gorge. "If Diego doesn't get the support he wants, rumor has it all the dams could go some night. That would turn everything around here into a big lake."

"What about the Romero place."

"Everything flooded, and the house uninhabitable."

She looked up at the white farmhouse. Its thick adobe walls seemed as solid and immovable as the mountains. But they weren't. Their walls were made of sun-dried bricks of mud and straw and would collapse if underwater for any length of time.

"Diego intimidates the local farmers, getting them to back him against Guevara. If they don't, things happen," Jake said. "Last month a rancher disappeared. Another had his small dam, upstream from here, fail in the middle of the night. That one little broken dam put a foot of water over hundreds of acres of corn and wheat and drowned a flock of sheep."

She left the rock, walked back and stood on the bank, leaning against a large willow tree. Looking out over the water, she asked, "How do they stop it?"

"By stopping Diego."

She shook her head. "Him again. It's all connected, isn't it? Diego, the Romeros, you, me, Lloyd."

He gave her a sharp look.

She pushed away from the tree and moved closer to him. "In last week's paper," she began, "Lloyd printed what General Diego threatened to do in this part of Chihuahua. I asked him where he got his information, but he wouldn't tell me. He ran an inch-high headline on page one: GUEVARA SENDS TROOPS. Under that were articles on threats to the dams and the possible overthrow of the Guevara regime."

"I read it," Jake said. "Diego, of course, denies everything. Lloyd gave away too much too soon. Diego is furious that his plans were leaked, and humiliated that an American newspaper published them. Now Mexican soldiers sent by the president are stationed along the river."

"Was my brother killed in retaliation for that article?" It was a question she didn't want to ask, being afraid the answer was yes, and yet she needed to know. Jake and his men had rushed into Mexico after her for a reason.

Jake stared out at the river, then shook his head. "I hope not."

"So the dams are safe for now?"

He nodded. "Because of the troops." He was silent for a moment, and then he turned and met her gaze directly. "When all this is over, you and I have to talk."

"Let's talk now."

He held his hand up. "I can't. Not yet."

She frowned. "Maria said you and Ricardo were scouts in the Cavalry, that you worked together."

"Sometimes we did. They call it Reconnaissance now."

"And when I'm kidnapped by Mexican soldiers, Texas Rangers come after me and hide me in a former spy-buddy's house. Am I seeing a connection here?"

"Later."

"You've met my brother, haven't you?"

Jake hesitated, then said, "Your brother was respected and well liked. So is your father. I took a delegation from our Ranger camp and Fort Bliss to his wife's funeral. A week or so after, Lloyd came out to the fort to see me. We had dinner together there, and at your house a couple of times. Once he had me bring Colonel Gordon with me to your house."

He stopped and gazed at her, his eyes unreadable—a blank look she'd come to despise, a look which locked everyone else out. Like an animal burrowing into its hole, he was gone. Would he lie to her? There was only one way to find out.

She took a deep breath. "Maria told me that Lloyd has been down here. Is that true?"

Jake dragged a hand down his face and sighed. "I brought him here to meet Ricardo."

"Why?"

"I was following orders, orders I believed in and still do. I thought by exposing what was going on here, Lloyd could help the United States and his fellow Texans avoid another confrontation with Mexico."

"Whose orders?"

"I can't answer that, but they came from very high up."

"And Ricardo?"

"The same. From someone high up in the Mexican government. Both countries want peace, Elizabeth."

"So if you hadn't introduced my brother to Ricardo, would he still be alive right now?" Her voice wobbled.

"I don't know the answer to that. I refused when he first asked me, but he went over my head." He paused, then added, "And then they came and kidnapped you."

"Coincidence?"

He shrugged. "As Rangers we're trained not to trust such things as coincidence. When I said I was going after you, things fell into place almost instantly. No problems getting into Mexico, and once we were there, we never saw a soldier until after we had taken you away from the Mexicans."

Jake shook his head. "I've said all I can say now. Let's put the rest of this conversation off until we get back home. Agreed?"

"For now," she said.

But in the back of her mind, questions were stirring, each

one demanding answers. From out of nowhere, doubts about him began assaulting her thoughts.

Who was Jake Nelson really?

Besides the little that Maria had shared about Jake's boyhood, everything else she knew about the man was what he himself had told her. He wasn't married, had been in the Cavalry, Special Forces, and the Frontier Battalion.

She nibbled her lip, trying to remember what she'd read about the Battalion. It was formed for two reasons only—Texas border patrol and Texas law enforcement. The Indians were mainly gone and not a problem anymore. The Battalion now concentrated on Mexican bandits and American outlaws, bank robbers, train robbers.

The Battalion, they said, was highly selective, so Jake Nelson must be very good at something.

Not much to go on, she thought.

She started back toward the house.

Jake caught up with her and walked alongside. He glanced up and frowned at the sky. "Wind's kicking up," he said. "Weather might not hold. I'd better get going."

"Did you really come back this morning just to talk to Ricardo?"

"To be honest, no. I rode back because I figured you needed me. When I left this morning, you looked like Ruthie did when I found her that day in Texas—one scared little girl. I couldn't leave you like that."

She turned away from him, looking in the direction of the house, disturbed that he'd read her so easily.

"You seem surprised that I came back," he said.

"I suppose I was afraid I'd never see you again, that you might have left me here for good."

"On purpose? Ever? Why would you think that?"

She shrugged. "I don't really know you, Jake. I don't know what to expect from you."

"So you expected the worst." The skin around his eyes tightened. He shot a hand out, yanked her into his arms, and crooked her chin up.

When his gaze slipped to her mouth, everything went very still inside her. Surely he wasn't going to—

Yes, he was!

It was an angry kiss, although whether angry at himself or at her, she couldn't tell. She tried to push him away, but his fingers were wound in her hair.

For an instant she felt a flash of fear.

Of him? No, not of him.

She was afraid of herself and the attraction building between them.

As if he'd read her thoughts, the pressure on her mouth eased. He slipped his palms around and cradled both sides of her face. Slowly, gently, a warm mouth covered hers again—an affectionate, drawn-out kiss, coaxing, not demanding.

She was aware of the man in her arms, of muscle under shirtsleeves, of the unyielding hardness of his chest.

He didn't hold her tight against him. Instead, he held only her face with his fingertips and kissed her again. He touched only her lips with his, softly, so tender she nearly wept.

Emotion welled inside her. Even as she told herself not to, she slid her arms around his neck. Eyes closed, turning her face with his, she kissed Jake Nelson back.

When the kiss ended, he wrapped her in an embrace and held her tight. It felt good. *He* felt good.

Finally her eyes drifted open again. The man in her arms looked as dazed as she felt. He shook his head as if to clear it, then let her go. He stepped back, looking down at her as though he'd never seen her before.

"Duchess, you are trouble," he said softly.

"Do you always manhandle women like that?" she said, shocked by her response to him.

He blew out a slow stream of air. "You said you didn't know what to expect from me. I decided to prove you right."

"Well, you did. You certainly surprised me."

He gave a short huff. "I think I surprised myself more."

With that, he spun around and started across the field to the trees where his horse was tied.

"You can be sure I'll be back," he called, swinging himself up into the saddle. Without a glance back at her, he rode away.

A gust of wind whipped her hair across her face. She raised a hand and held it back, away from her eyes, and watched him ride up the hill with a sense of relief. He slowed the horse for a moment, shouted something to Ricardo at the barn, and galloped off.

∞

Head bowed, Ricardo prayed over the food set before them on the big round table. "*Bendíganos a Señor y estos tus regalos, que estamos a punto de recibir de tu prima, por Cristo nuestro Señor, Amén.*" Bless us, O Lord, in these thy gifts which we are about to receive from thy bounty through Christ our Lord. Amen.

Elizabeth listened, adding silent words of her own to his prayer. She wasn't praying for the blessing of food. She was asking the Lord for guidance, for anything to help her deal with a man she didn't understand, a man who disturbed her.

For Maria's sake, she pretended an interest in dinner. Maria had fixed a wonderful meal—a heaping platter of tender lamb chops, potatoes, and a cast-iron kettle of corn, onions, and red peppers.

Fred was thoroughly enjoying the spread of food and told Maria so every time he passed his plate for more.

Meanwhile, Elizabeth's thoughts chased around in her head, returning again and again, not to the meal but to a man on a big gray horse, racing away from her as fast as he could go.

If he was that anxious to get away, why did he kiss her?

And why in the world did she kiss him back?

She was under no illusions that she was important. This whole operation was driven by one country's—perhaps two countries'—desire to avoid war.

Like a chess piece, she was only a pawn in a game with high stakes. She felt vulnerable, unsure of herself in these unfamiliar surroundings. She desperately wished she were home—in Washington, in her own house, in her own room.

Fighting a sudden wave of homesickness, she wondered how her father was handling everything. By now, he knew about Lloyd and probably about her, too. He would be frantic and on his way west as fast as he could get here. She loved him dearly, her heart aching for him.

She looked up when a clock chimed somewhere in the house.

Jake had said he'd be back for her, but what if he couldn't come back? What he was doing was dangerous. Anything could happen. He could be captured or killed.

A cold feeling spread through her chest.

Of course he was coming back.

She closed her eyes in a long blink. *Look after him, Lord.*

Elizabeth scolded herself. For a moment this afternoon, she'd forgotten who Jake Nelson was, *what* he was—a Texas Ranger—and he, not she, controlled this operation. His kiss had underscored that for her in big red letters.

A mistake.

And kissing him back was the biggest mistake of all.

She got out of her chair and excused herself, explaining she had a headache and she needed to lie down. She thanked Maria for the meal and said good night to Ricardo and Fred. Dejected, she started up the stairs to her bedroom.

Once back in Texas, she'd never see Jake Nelson again—which was exactly the way she wanted it.

Still, she had to admit he was attractive in a muscular sort of way, not pretty like some men she knew. In fact, most women would declare Jake Nelson handsome, if they liked the physical type, that is. She, however, preferred brains over brawn any day.

"Señora?" Ricardo called up to her.

She turned and looked down at him.

"Jake said to expect him back in three days, five at the most. And though he didn't say what for, he said to tell you he was *not* sorry."

Of course he wasn't, she thought. Why should he be? He was probably having a great laugh at her expense. If she kissed him back, it was only out of gratitude for getting her away from the Mexicans. That's all.

She thanked Ricardo and continued up the stairs to her

room and flung herself onto the bed. So, big bad Jake wasn't sorry for kissing her, was he?

The rat.

She threw her arm over her eyes and let out a long sigh. Well, she certainly was.

She pulled the pillow over her face.

If she wasn't, she ought to be. Her throat tightened.

Please, God. I don't want to be hurt again.

∽

Lying in her bedroom in the Romero house, a soft breeze billowed the white lace curtain hanging over the small window. A shiver rippled down her spine as she reflected back to when her husband was alive. Jake Nelson and Carl Evans had been cut from the same piece of cloth—both towheads, both Texans, both living on the edge of danger and loving it. Like Carl, Jake exuded that same cocky confidence that came from risking his neck and surviving.

She'd met Carl Evans four years earlier in Washington, on the steps of the Capitol where her senator father worked. The steely-nerved Cavalry Lieutenant Carl Evans from Fort Myer, Virginia, had just given a talk to enlistment officers that Fourth of July in 1882. She'd been hurrying down the steps to hail a carriage when her heel went out from under her and she fell into him, knocking the books and papers out of his hand.

Embarrassed, she'd gone down on her knees to gather up the papers from the steps before they blew away.

"I'm so sorry," she'd mumbled to the pair of uniformed knees stooping beside her, then looked up into a pair of vivid blue eyes and a smile that could melt a snowball half a block away.

"I'm not," the lieutenant said, grinning.

In between one breath and the next, practical, levelheaded Elizabeth Madison fell in love. Completely. With all her heart. That day, she and Carl slipped off together, riding streetcars, hopping off to explore, and holding hands and kissing when no one was looking. One snowy December morning five months later, she married him. In the spring she moved west with him to Fort Quitman, Texas, when his unit was reassigned.

They'd been like a couple of kids playing house, living on post. Her cooking, cleaning, and running to meet him, and Carl coming through the door, laughing, swinging her around, so full of life he crackled.

She breathed a painful, fractured sigh. Like autumn leaves, other pictures scattered across her mind: the sad, sorrowful train ride to Dallas seven months later to take him home, his family, her family, the sea of dress uniforms, the regal bronze casket draped in red, white, and blue.

Taps.

Elizabeth rolled over in the bed and gazed at the white lace curtain, hanging now limp and still, an icy little hole where her heart had been.

Eight

JAKE HAD BEEN IN SAN JOSE the year before, and the village looked as if it hadn't changed at all since then. Time appeared to have stopped here long ago. White mud and stone houses filled the narrow streets with stepped sidewalks. Iron balconies with pots of flowers overhung steep streets that, only two generations earlier, had echoed with the hoofbeats of the Church's inquisitors.

All streets led to the village square, a paved area featuring a fountain at the center, and an arcade that bordered three of its sides—a roofed walkway jutting out from the buildings, which provided relief to shoppers against the wind and storms and the searing sun. Grateful to get away from the fierceness of the hot, dry wind, Jake strolled along the arcade, peering into the store windows as he passed.

Wooden buildings with signs and storefronts crowded together. He saw the same tired bank, the stage stop, and two saloons. Beyond were the pool halls and more stores. And between the bank and another pool hall was the Western Union Telegraph Office.

Two old men in caps sat on a bench by a store window

and nodded as he walked past them. A widow, dressed in lifelong black, hurried across the square, shaking her finger at boys playing pelota against the side of the church at the end of the square.

Next to a meat market with a crate of live chickens in the window, he found a café. He ducked inside and took a table facing the door so he could watch for Gus. He hadn't eaten since early that morning and was famished. The lunch he'd planned to eat at the Romero house had never happened.

Because after he kissed Elizabeth, he ran.

Ran like a horse with its tail on fire. That kiss—and his unexpected reaction to it—had shaken him. He was at a loss to explain how he felt. Or why.

He snapped his head around at the faint scuff of a shoe alongside him, startled he hadn't heard the person approach. He tensed and glanced up to see the café owner, a tray in hand, waiting to take his order. Disturbed at his inattention, Jake quickly read the list of that day's offering of food, scrawled on a slate hanging on the wall. He gave his order in crisp Mexican Spanish.

As the man disappeared through a curtain of clicking glass beads, Jake wondered if he'd been wrong to wave off Ricardo's suggestion of a bodyguard. Yet, deep down, Jake knew he was right. Another man tagging along would have made them all suspect.

The café owner returned and set in front of him a small crusty loaf of bread, a bowl of spicy chicken broth with onions and hominy, and a dish of plump black olives.

Slowly the knot in his belly loosened. The spicy broth warmed him and helped him relax. He tried to force his thoughts in another direction.

It had been a couple of hours since he'd left Elizabeth, and he still couldn't get her out of his mind. He could kick himself for kissing her.

Still tense from that good-bye, he blew out a breath of air. Shaking his head slightly, he broke off a chunk of bread and wondered what he'd missed. Her words said one thing, her eyes another. And her kiss said something he still couldn't quite believe.

He soon finished the soup and then began picking at the olives.

A muscle ticked in his cheek.

She didn't mean it.

She couldn't mean it.

But what if she did?

He didn't understand it. For some reason, women were very friendly toward Texas Rangers and hung all over them at bars and gambling tables. Every town was the same that way. Just knowing they were Rangers drew women, when it should have warned them away. Rangers were lousy husband material, himself included.

Permanent relationships and Jake Nelson: the two didn't mix. In the last decade, he'd told a lot of women good-bye. The Army made that easy. Ten long years had passed and he hadn't allowed himself to get attached to any girl. Safer that way, although homecomings sometimes gave him a twinge.

When they returned from an operation, his fellow Rangers were met with squealing hugs and kisses from their wives and children, families jumping up and down with excitement.

But nobody was there to meet him.

And yet women were a fixture in his life, one pretty

girl after another parading through his world. Women he soon forgot. Several times he pretended he cared, hoping somehow it might turn out to be true. It never did. Now, when it looked as though a relationship was heading in a serious direction, he ran the other way, broke it off before anyone got hurt.

Before *he* got hurt.

He didn't want to be pressured into something he wasn't ready for, might never be ready for again.

Like marriage.

There was a time, long ago, when he thought he was ready, thought he'd met the perfect girl, Audrey Simmons, who worked as a seamstress, a respected position. He bought her a ring and started making plans to build a life together, a real family.

But then one night his superiors at headquarters miscalculated and sent him and a sixty-man command to attack an Apache camp of hundreds, armed with bows and rifles and waiting for them.

The soldiers were quickly outnumbered and outflanked, forced into a three-hour fighting retreat. He lost six men that night, including his best friend. His horse was shot from under him, and Jake took a bullet in the upper arm trying to find another mount. Running, jumping, he caught the bridle of a dead soldier's horse and threw himself into the saddle.

Knowing the men were watching, he raised his rifle over his head, waved for them to follow, then took off at a gallop. Standing in the stirrups, he let out a shout that was heard for half a mile. The men followed him, riding hard and yelling like banshees.

Jake was strong for them. He had to be.

After the hospital at Fort Richardson patched them up, they gave the wounded a few days' leave. Jake left at once. He wanted Audrey, his fiancée. Rubbed raw inside and hurting, he needed to talk to her, to hold her.

To *be* held.

He rode all night to get to her, trotting into the yard of her little house just outside town before sunup. The flat calm that always followed a firefight had long since disappeared, replaced by muscle tremors and a wound-too-tight feeling. That too would pass, he knew, as soon as he wrapped his arms around her.

Knowing she'd be up soon to go to work for the dress-maker, he quietly entered the kitchen through the back door and went to the stove to put on a pot of coffee. Everything took longer with his arm in a sling. When the coffee was ready, he poured himself a cup and sipped slowly.

A few minutes later, he looked up when her bedroom door opened and Audrey came out, dressed for work.

Her eyes widened.

Jake jumped up so fast he knocked his chair over.

Right behind her walked a barefooted marine, button-ing his shirt.

Jake was so taken aback by the sight, he thought he'd die right then.

A loud argument followed. The marine grabbed the rest of his clothes and lit out for the door. It wasn't the first time, Audrey admitted. There'd been others—men in his own company, men who reported to him, men who had respected him.

Hearing her confession, his jaw dropped. Inside him,

something was running away, tunneling deeper, trying to hide. He sank into a chair and bit down the anger burning a hole in his gut.

She accused him of not loving her—not enough anyway. "Your men are more important to you than I am," she said.

"They have to be!" he shouted. "My job is to keep them alive."

"Then I've changed my mind. I don't *want* to be an Army wife." She pulled off her engagement ring and dropped it on the table.

He scooped the ring up and thrust it into his pocket. "You won't be! Not mine, anyway."

At that moment, like blowing out a candle, he stopped loving her.

Outside, mounted on his horse again, he dragged his good hand down his face, surprised to find his cheeks wet. He swallowed hard.

Officers don't cry.

He pulled out a handkerchief and dried his eyes.

∽

Last month, before Elizabeth was kidnapped, Jake and Colonel Gordon had spent a couple of hours relaxing and talking, discussing Texas and the Army. Tieless, shirt unbuttoned at the neck, Colonel Gordon slouched in an armchair, chewing on a cigar. Jake sat in a chair opposite the colonel, his boots propped on a footstool. He yawned and grunted sleepily.

Gordon smiled. All that casualness and good humor was deceptive. In truth, Jake Nelson was cool and remote, difficult to get close to. The profile Gordon had worked up on him revealed a man who hated to lose, who hated being second best in anything.

Jake took no unnecessary chances with his men and refused to budge until all the pieces of an operation were in place. Then there was no holding him back. Not everyone liked him, but when it came to his judgment of things, the men trusted Jake fully and would follow him anywhere. He was a leader.

And that was exactly why the Frontier Battalion had gone after him three years before. And why Colonel Gordon was about to do the same.

That afternoon, Gordon and a committee from Defense Intelligence had selected Nelson for an assignment. Gordon was looking for a new Executive Officer qualified to head up the Fourth Cavalry Regiment. He knew Jake well, knew that Jake would want hard information to come to a decision. Any convincing to be done must come from within himself.

Gordon stood and walked to the window. He looked out and gestured to the wide parade ground below. "I know you've heard the rumors about what's ahead for this fort. They're not rumors," he said quietly. "They're enlarging Fort Bliss beyond anything we've heard. We are going to be one of the biggest installations in the country. We're fine now, but in a few months things are going to break wide open. We will have more men, horses, and equipment than we can handle. I'd like for you to come work with me. I need a good XO. Your time with the Texas Rangers is almost up. Can we persuade you to come back to the U.S. Army and help run this battalion?"

Hands in his pockets, the colonel turned around and faced Jake. "Incidentally, that's *Major* if you accept."

∞

The spring bell over the front door jangled. Jake looked up as Gus walked in. He saw Jake and chuckled. "You look ready to shoot someone," he said.

Jake forced a laugh and pulled out the chair next to him. "Not at all. Sit down. You get us a place to stay tonight?"

"Around the corner in a boardinghouse, second floor."

"Learn anything yet?"

Gus nodded and looked around. Except for two young people buying candy, the café was empty now. "About an hour after I left you and Fred this morning, a Mexican major with a scarred face went pounding by me at a dead run on the road to San Jose, same road you came in on."

"That would've been Major Chavez," Jake said. "What else?"

"He turned back, stopped and asked if I'd seen anyone. I said I'd seen only one man with two cows. When I told him that, he just nodded, waved, and raced off toward San Jose again. I figured he'd already seen the same man I did."

"I also saw the man with the cows on the way here. Was one of those cows mostly black with a big white spot on its hind end?"

Gus nodded. "Almost the whole leg was white."

Frowning, Jake leaned back in his chair and ran two fingers across his mouth. Facts were adding up. "The man we saw with the cows is probably a sentry for the Mexicans," he said. "My guess is the Army's keeping tabs on who is going to and from San Jose right now. That tells us somebody important is either here or coming here—a stroke of luck for us."

Finished with his meal, Jake tossed two coins onto the table and stood up to leave. He looked back over his shoulder at the owner. "Gracias, señor," he said, and followed Gus outside.

∽

In serapes and sombreros, sashes knotted about their waists, Jake and Gus roamed San Jose, shopped the stores, and had a horse re-shod, sizing up the town and its inhabitants. They wore their trouser legs out over their boots to look more like vaqueros, Mexican cowboys who sometimes rode barefoot. Knee-high boots laced over pant legs was an American look, a Ranger look. Jake and Gus were both fluent in Mexican Spanish, and Jake could color his words anytime he chose with the peculiar Chihuahuan accent.

While looking around the livery stable, two columns of soldiers passed quickly through town, their eyes straight ahead. In the middle were six horses with loaded saddles, roped together in single-file. Each saddle mound was tied to the horse and carefully covered with a blanket.

Jake looked at Gus. It wasn't hard to figure out what those blankets covered.

On a secret scouting assignment over the border last year, they'd surprised a Mexican patrol and lost three Rangers in a nighttime shootout. He wouldn't—couldn't—leave them there without risking a war. He called the mission off and ran for the border, along with the fallen Rangers tied across the saddles of their own horses. And he swore those horses knew. Not one of them raised their heads the whole trip back.

This column seemed headed for a small Mexican outpost five miles from San Jose.

A heavyset man whose blue uniform jacket bristled with medals rode in the second group, following the advance patrol clearing the way through town.

Jake said softly to Gus, "Recognize him?"

Gus nodded, his face tight. "Diego. I've seen him before. His men are well trained and loyal. Most are afraid of him and who he knows."

"And look who's with him."

"Major Chavez himself."

"The two of them together locks it up. Two positive identifications—yours and mine. That's good enough," Jake said, and watched the last of the column turn south out of San Jose. "Let's stay tonight and see what else we learn. Then tomorrow we'll get our lady friend and head home—fast, before they start looking for us."

Nine

EARLY THE NEXT MORNING, Elizabeth answered a tap on the door. Smiling, Maria stood in the hall with a cup of coffee, looking as if she'd been up for hours.

"The boys are off at school and Ricardo is working in the barn. How about we go into town? I'll introduce you to the priest and show you around their orphanage. I teach there three mornings a week, and today is one of my days."

Two hours later, shielding her eyes, Elizabeth gazed at a walled compound of buildings climbing a hillside. Except for an ancient bell tower dominating the corner overlooking the village, it might have been a fortress. It seemed completely out of place in this quiet Mexican countryside.

San Miguel was a small community in the foothills of the Sierra Madre. From a distance, the whitewashed mud houses looked swept together against the mountain, their tile roofs touching. A sandstone church with a modest cross stood at one end of a large arcaded square; the school the two Romero boys attended, at the other.

"That's our monastery, San Miguel," Maria said proudly. "The building off to the left is the orphanage the Benedictines run. I teach English there a couple of days a week. Jakina's from there. When we couldn't find her parents, Ricardo and I adopted her. She was left there one morning as a tiny infant."

Church bells tolled, a deep, loud clanging, slow and insistent. Elizabeth looked up at the bell tower and blinked. Maria laughed. "That's the call to midmorning prayers. All the monks inside are running to the abbey. Funny. They're just like us—always late."

"Not all of them. Just the young ones," a voice said from behind. "We older men usually watch the clock better."

Maria spun around, smiling. "But not today, Father, eh?"

She turned to Elizabeth and Fred Barkley, who had come along. "Father Lorenzo is the abbot of San Miguel, and he's going to be late if he doesn't get going."

"Right you are. Are you teaching this morning?" Father Lorenzo asked. When Maria nodded, he said, "I'll see you all inside, then."

When the bells stopped, the air quivering in the sudden silence, Father Lorenzo broke into a jog for the gate, black robe swirling at his heels.

Maria turned left and led them to the massive front door. Fred pushed it open and followed the women into the vaulted lobby ahead of them.

Dim inside, the stone monastery held an air of gloominess, as if even the sun had given up trying to penetrate the place. The heavy aroma of incense hung in the air. They crossed the granite floor of the lobby, footsteps echoing.

"Good morning, Maria." A tall monk called from the long counter off to one side. His ankle-length black robe was tied around the waist, its hood lying in folds across his shoulders. A circle of scalp was shaved bare on the crown of his head.

Fred and Elizabeth followed Maria outside and down a sheltered walkway bordered by marble pillars. The stained-glass windows of the abbey ahead sparkled in the sunlight.

Black-robed men crisscrossed the courtyard to the abbey at the other end. Most nodded pleasantly to them but said nothing as they passed.

Deep male chanting drifted out from the abbey.

Maria led Fred and Elizabeth to a bench alongside the cloister wall. "Would you like to sit for a minute and listen?"

Elizabeth nodded, sat and leaned back and let the sweet, solemn music wash over her. She closed her eyes and said a quiet thank-you to God. For the first time in days, she didn't feel like crying. She hadn't realized how much she needed this, she thought, and listened to the men singing psalms.

With a long sigh she stood a few minutes later, and the three of them left the cloister to go to Maria's English class.

The orphanage was a large adobe building with its own living quarters behind San Miguel. The schoolrooms overlooked the mountains. Maria's classroom was a sunny room with a blackboard and two long desks for the students, all girls under ten. Their parents had either died or disappeared, and neighbors brought them to the monks. Two of the girls had been abandoned as infants.

There was a piano in the room, and Elizabeth played softly in the background while Maria read the story of Snow White aloud to the class. A low, sour chord accompanied the evil stepmother in the story, and each of the dwarfs had their own silly combination of notes. Even

Fred got into it, jumping to his feet with a hand over his heart every time the handsome prince was mentioned. It was a fun hour of learning and laughter heard all over the building.

Before the class ended, a beaming Father Lorenzo stopped by and invited the grown-ups to have lunch with him in his office.

∽

"Uh-oh."

As soon as she walked into Father Lorenzo's office, Elizabeth saw Jake standing at the window. Head slumped, hands braced on either side of the window frame, he stared out blankly. Gus, eyes closed, was sprawled in a chair. Both of them wore their pants outside their boots.

Jake wheeled around when the office door opened.

"I didn't . . ." Her voice trailed, searching for a different word.

"Expect me so soon?" he finished for her. "You never know with me." A corner of his mouth dug in, hiding a smile.

"I'm glad you find my expectations amusing."

He grinned outright.

She stiffened. "I assume the fact that you're here is not a good sign."

"That's right."

With a thoughtful look at Maria, he added, "We saw Ricardo this morning on our way back. Mexican soldiers are going house to house asking about an American woman and three Rangers. We're not going back with you today. Too risky for you and Ricardo."

Elizabeth's face paled. "What are we going to do?"

"What the Mexicans did bringing you down here—sleep outside. Or find another cave. And get out of this country fast."

Father Lorenzo took his glasses off and tapped them on the desk. "Let's think a minute." He looked at Elizabeth. "Jake and I go back a few years to when Ricardo and Maria named him godfather to Jakina. Since non-Catholics cannot be godparents to a Catholic child, we settled for *unofficial* godfather. Before you came in this morning, he explained why you're here, why he's here, and the danger you are both in. What is going on in our beloved Mexico with these dams and General Diego will reflect badly on our government."

Father Lorenzo walked around the desk. "However, we may be able to help. In the 1600s, this abbey was a refuge, a secret sanctuary for dissidents. Although it's been a few years, we still welcome dissidents from time to time. We'd be honored to have you stay with us in our guest rooms." He looked around with a broad smile. "It appears that history is repeating itself."

Jake walked over and shook Lorenzo's hand. "Thank you. That gives us time to make plans. But are you sure we won't be putting you at risk?"

"There's no risk for San Miguel," Father Lorenzo said. "Until this budding revolt of General Diego's is resolved one way or the other, this regime has given orders to keep hands off all churches. That will no doubt change in the future, but right now they don't want to stir us up." He chuckled. "Their main concern is keeping the Church quiet. Our relationship with the government is a stormy one."

∞

Their rooms were on the third floor of a small complex behind the monastery. Jake had selected a corner room with a window overlooking the courtyard and valley below. At the end of the hall was another set of stairs, giving them two escape routes if needed.

Elizabeth stood in her guest room, looking around. The floor had a woven rag rug in the center. A small fireplace took up one corner, the bed and dresser taking up the rest of the room.

Jake came up behind her and squeezed her shoulder lightly. With a gasp she whirled around.

"Relax," he said. "You're as jumpy as I am."

She swallowed and huffed a short breath. "You've never been jumpy in your life."

Jake went to the window and looked out. "I have the room next door, but you'll have company in here. The three of us will take turns sitting on the floor inside the door. Just a precaution." He held his hand up. "I know, I know. Back home, people would be scandalized, but they'll never know unless you tell them. In similar circumstances they'd do exactly the same. It eliminates any risk of your being taken again. None of us want that."

Hands in his pockets, he rocked back and forth on his heels. "Diego is going to tear Chihuahua apart looking for you. That makes me very jumpy. He can't let you leave the country."

Elizabeth stared at him. "You're scaring me."

"I'm sorry, but you need to know. Let's go eat and take your mind off things."

"Give me five minutes to wash up and put myself together."

"You look fine," he said quietly. "You always look fine."

She snapped a glance at him, thinking he was being sarcastic, but he turned away and said no more.

Ten

The Next Morning

As usual, Father Lorenzo rose before dawn and went to the window. It would soon be light.

After lunch yesterday, when he'd recovered his composure at having three heavily armed Texas Rangers and an American senator's abducted daughter in his monastery, he set about getting the weapons out of sight. "Forgive an old man," he told them, "but they make me uncomfortable. And, I suspect, probably the brothers, as well."

Jake hadn't hesitated. "I understand completely. Where would you like us to put them?"

"Leave them here in my office until you're ready to leave. They won't be touched. No one uses this room but me."

Immediately three men unbuckled heavy holsters, slid rifles off their shoulders, pulled out knives, more revolvers, and two sticks of something that looked like dynamite. They laid them on a table by the window. Each one of them, however, had a small revolver tucked out of sight, inside a pocket or boot or under an arm.

Father Lorenzo looked at the weapons, then at the three Rangers standing in his office. "Our souls, unfortunately, have no such armor. All they have to defend themselves—and us—is faith."

He extended an invitation to attend mass that evening, if they were so inclined. To his delight, his message got through. Coming out of the abbey after Vespers that evening, he saw Ranger Gus Dukker and hurried to catch up with him.

"I'm so pleased to see you," Lorenzo said. "What made you decide to come?"

"Guilt, Father," Gus mumbled.

"Why guilt, my son?"

"I haven't been to mass in five years. Got to thinking maybe my soul could use some of that ammunition you talked about."

Father Lorenzo smiled and said, "Welcome back. *He* missed you."

∽

Lorenzo carried his coffee to the window to watch the sun come up. This was his time of the day, a gift from the Lord.

The jagged peaks of the Sierra Madre rose nearly two miles high into a purple morning sky. The eastern horizon glowed, lit from below. Crimson and corals streaked upward, blushing the snowcaps, the clouds, and reddening the sky itself.

Lorenzo took a long, thoughtful sip of his coffee. If the old saying was right, bad weather was on the way.

Rain coming.

From watching them all these many years, he'd come to

know what the cloud shapes and height and their changing colors meant. From years of observing, he now knew that when his eyesight sharpened and he could read without his spectacles, the barometer was falling, and he'd better take his umbrella. One of the advantages of getting older was the ability to read the small signs in life of what lay ahead.

This killing of another Texas newspaper editor by Mexicans—the second in five years, and only a few miles from the first—would go badly for the government. Added to that was the kidnapping of the editor's sister, the daughter of a prominent American senator. The combination of those two events might finally topple General Diego. Especially after what Lorenzo had recently learned. Spread open on the desk behind him was Lloyd Madison's *Grande Examiner*, revealing Diego's takeover plot.

Lorenzo stared at the sky, trying to read it—or read between the lines, if there were any—as to which way it would all go.

In another couple of days, all Mexico would know what was happening—unless General Diego could catch the Americans before they crossed the Rio Grande.

And that must not happen.

Father Lorenzo looked at the mountains and the crimson skies behind them, and breathed a prayer that the Texas Rangers could get Señora Evans and themselves out of Mexico before it was too late.

Eleven

"ELIZABETH, YOU ALL RIGHT?" Gus called.

Jake hipped around in his saddle. "Why? What's wrong with her?"

"Looks like the altitude's getting to her. I feel it some myself," Gus said.

Jake chided himself. He should've been watching her closer. But that morning they'd all been rushing, pushed along by an uneasy sense that time was running out.

When Maria showed up on horseback at San Miguel at the usual time for her class that morning, two monks were waiting for her. They took her horse to the stables and watched the doors while three Rangers and Elizabeth unpacked the saddlebags and reloaded them into the bags on Elizabeth's new horse, purchased from the monastery a few hours before. Her original little Mexican horse had a brand and a serial number, and would be easily identified if they were stopped. As soon as they were loaded, they left San Miguel and rode all day. Occasionally they broke into a gallop for a change of pace for a mile or two to make up time.

Jake hoped to reach the Rio Grande tomorrow morning

and cross over before noon. Now, he dropped back and reined his horse alongside hers. Eyes narrowed, he studied her. Mountain sickness—headache, out of breath—the first signs.

The first time he'd looked at her photograph, he thought he had her pegged. A senator's daughter, classy and rich and spoiled. Yet he was wrong. She wasn't spoiled. Not once had she complained about anything.

"You look pale. How do you feel?" he asked.

"I'm fine. Have a teeny little headache, that's all." She let out a breathy laugh.

A week ago, that might have fooled him into thinking she was all right. Now he knew her better. Physically, and probably emotionally as well, she was on the edge. But her pride wouldn't let her show it. Jake pulled out his canteen and passed it over to her, watching her swallow. She was used to sea level, not riding and working a horse at eight thousand feet elevation. Because she was on the small side, so was her bloodstream, and it simply couldn't carry enough oxygen to support her.

He regretted that they'd come up to this height so fast, partly because she'd enjoyed those little gallops. She was turning into a decent rider.

Climbing fast was why she was so out of breath and tired.

He stretched and grunted. "We've gone far enough for one day. Suppose we look around up here, find some wood and water, and make camp."

When she gave a sigh of relief and turned away, he knew he'd made the right decision.

They followed a rocky trail that wound around a sheer cliff rising on one side, the face wet with trickles of mountain snowmelt. Jake suddenly reined to a stop and seized her arm.

The men exchanged glances. They all smelled it.

Smoke.

Keeping Elizabeth behind them, the Rangers slowly began walking their horses. Ahead lay a wide clearing, hemmed in by low reddish orange cliffs cut with openings, a honeycomb of caves. A faint haze drifted across the ridgeline. The smoke must have come from cookstoves within the mountain.

"*Gitanos*," Jake said. Gypsies.

The trail ran through the center of their camp, past the caves. Tents and shacks dotted the area, along with Gypsy vans and decorated wagons—*vardos*. The men sat in the tent openings and wagon doorways and watched a group of children fighting and playing among themselves. The children rushed around them, begging for money, pulling at their saddlebags. One boy snatched Jake's hat off, but Jake shot a hand out and snatched it back.

A teenage girl darted in and grabbed the scarf off Elizabeth's head. The loose braid tucked under it came apart and long hair fell out. Elizabeth made a swipe for the scarf, but the girl ran away, laughing at her.

Near the trail, a man approached the horses, clapping his hands and whistling to the animals. He seemed displeased to see strangers in the camp. His face hardened as the four riders pulled to a stop.

"*Buenas tardes, señor*," Jake said. "We're not here to make trouble. We are just passing through."

"You *la policía*?" the man asked.

Jake and Fred both laughed. "No, no," Jake said. "We are not police."

The man grinned. "Then I guess you must be running

113

from them. Buenas tardes! I am Laszlo. Please don't mind the children, señor—they were just playing."

Gus slid off his horse and said in Romani, "*Sastipe, sar sal?*" Hello, how are you?

Laszlo said, "You speak Romani?"

"A little. My grandmother's Romani." Gus stuck his hand out. "*May buchhov* Gus Dukker."

Laszlo stepped forward with a smile, a flash of white teeth in a swarthy face. He pumped Gus's hand. "*Bor*—you are one of us."

Gus laughed. "Almost."

Laszlo nodded to Elizabeth and translated for her and the others. "*Devlesa avilan*—It is God who brought you here," he said. "You are safe here. Like you, *Comandante*, we have no love for the police or the army or Diego and his death squads."

"You know who we are, then?" Jake asked.

"*Sí.* They are looking everywhere for three Rangers and a woman. Your enemies call you *El Oso Amarillo*, the yellow bear. When your hat came off and I saw your hair, then hers, I knew it was you." He extended his hand. "Welcome, *mi amigo*, El Oso Amarillo. Tell me, why have the Rangers never talked to us? We Gypsies can find out things that might be helpful." His face darkened. "Our allegiance is to ourselves, not to the government or to anyone else. But we will do you the courtesy of listening."

Jake looked at him and blinked. Talking to Gypsies had never occurred to him. The Mexicans despised them. As a result, Gypsies stayed alert and had developed a talent for discovering facts and information others often missed. For them, it was a means of self-preservation.

"You're right—we should have talked to you long before this," Jake said. "But if all goes well, we won't be needing your help. If it does not, then we'll be back soon. That's a promise."

Laszlo clapped him on the shoulder and led them all toward a blue and yellow vardo, warning them about the soldiers on the roads. Although his vardo was small inside, it was divided into two rooms: the kitchen-living room and the sleeping quarters.

With the windows open, it was remarkably airy and cool inside and spotlessly clean.

A dark-haired woman with a baby on her hip stirred a blue-enameled pot on a small stove. With a smile, Laszlo introduced them all.

"Gracias, señora," Jake said, nodding to Laszlo's wife, Nadia. In English, he told Elizabeth, "On the way over, her husband said the road north is crawling with Mexican troops. He invited us to stay the night, said they'll find a place for us. They know who we are."

"Great," Elizabeth said. "I'm so hungry, and she's cooking something over there in that pot that smells heavenly."

<hr />

Humming to herself, Elizabeth sat down at the little folding table in the kitchen. Knees and shoulders touching, she, Jake, Laszlo, Nadia, and their two children all crowded together. Fred and Gus sat cross-legged on the floor, plates in their laps. Six adults and two children squeezed into the five-by-ten-foot space.

Nadia had fixed a *cocido*—a pinto, black, and garbanzo bean stew with chunks of rabbit, corn, potatoes, and any other vegetables she found in her kitchen. A flat, salty corn cake and a pitcher of wild-tasting goat's milk finished off the menu.

"Delicious. I've never tasted goat's milk before," Elizabeth said, licking her lips. She raised an eyebrow at Jake who, after one tiny sip, carefully set his glass down.

Elizabeth smiled at his expression. She leaned over and patted his hand. For a few hours at least, life had returned to normal.

They took turns, passing the nine-month-old baby from lap to lap and feeding her with their fingers from their plates.

Elizabeth looked over at Jake as he let the baby lick his fingers. His face was different, soft and half smiling, the cleft in his chin deepening. He leaned back in his chair and gave Elizabeth a long, bored look.

Liar, she thought. Reaching out, she rested her hand on his forearm and felt the muscles tighten beneath his shirt-sleeve. Despite that easy, casual attitude, he was as tense as she was. She wondered if she'd ever understand a man whose eyes told her one thing but whose lips said something quite different.

He acted as if he were three different men rolled up into one.

His public image was that of the dedicated Ranger—in control, determined, a man with all the charm of a wolf about to spring on its prey. That one strode into a roomful of men and held a gun on them, brazenly taking charge. That one raised the hair on the back of her neck.

Then there was the serious man who smiled easily when around friends, as comfortable with judges and abbots as he was with cowboys. An officer who joined the Rangers and took up the cause for justice because nobody else would. If he stayed in the Army, he'd probably wind up running it.

And finally—her throat tightened—there was the private Jake Nelson, the man she'd only caught glimpses of when he momentarily dropped the mask. The toughness disappeared then, replaced by a gentleness no one knew he possessed. That one had kissed her with such exquisite tenderness she'd nearly wept.

Who was he now? she wondered.

∞

As soon as the meal was over, they all followed Nadia outside, dragging their chairs and cushions with them and arranging them in a semicircle around the front of the vardo.

When Nadia went back inside for another pillow, Elizabeth said softly to Jake, "Do all Gypsies live like this?"

He nodded. "Most of them. They're treated like pariahs everywhere, here and in the U.S. No one trusts them; they can't get jobs."

"Ever have any work for you?" she asked, watching the open door of the vardo for Nadia.

"Not in the Rangers."

"Why not?"

"Mainly because they can't qualify. To join the Rangers, you must own a good horse, saddle, the best weapons. That all costs money, which most Gypsies don't have. Also, they have a reputation as being the best thieves and pickpockets in the world. I don't know as I believe it—I never wanted to take the chance. But now I think I would."

He returned a big wave to Laszlo, who was walking up and down the rows of vardos inviting everyone to come meet his new friends from Texas.

To Elizabeth's surprise, they came almost at once. The word was out. The Texas Rangers were among them. Still, they acted wary, for most of them had never seen, let alone talked to, a Texas Ranger.

Handsome, sharp-eyed men led their wives and families over to see what kind of man he was.

In Texas, they were The Law.

At first, the questions came at Jake slowly, and then one after the other, questions about the government—Mexican as well as American. Jake answered them all. Questions about the Rangers, about how much money he made, about his family. When they asked about his father, he explained how they used to fight, all the drinking, and his leaving home when he was fifteen. "Not good," he said.

Gypsy faces softened. A few men nodded and moved closer, appreciating his honesty. They understood. Many of them had similar childhoods.

Elizabeth was moved as well as she heard him speak of his background.

Answering a question about defensive tactics, he drew diagrams with a stick in the dirt. When he finished, he drove the stick into the ground and pointed to them and then to himself. "We need each other," he said.

Off to one side with the women, Elizabeth watched him and was puzzled by what she saw. The man was a born leader, she thought. With a sudden flash of insight, she realized that Jake viewed these men as potential allies and possible recruits. She smiled to herself.

She'd been raised in Washington, D.C. She could pick it up instantly when a man was politicking. Jake might not know it himself, but she did. Captain Jake Nelson was campaigning for votes and approval when and if he ever needed them, and doing a fine job of it. No matter what he said, he belonged in government.

As it grew dark, the guitars came out and the music began. A large campfire had been built, which was circled now by many, including Jake. Arms folded, standing close to the fire, he talked with a group of men. Brassy shadows from the fire flickered across his face.

The warm sound of guitars playing filled the air as the throbbing beat of flamenco began and the castanets *click-click-click*ed. Soon the guitars grew louder, faster, raspier.

Glasses filled to the brim with a dark purple wine appeared on brass trays. Elizabeth smiled her thanks when someone pressed a glass into her hand. She sipped, tasting it. Wonderful. Fragrant.

She glanced at Jake. He was surrounded by women, pretty women with long hair who were obviously flirting with him. He bent toward them, listening attentively as they spoke and laughed. Elizabeth drained her glass and turned her attention to the dancers.

The Gypsies kept time, clapping hands and stamping feet, beating out the vibrant rhythm. Elizabeth was fascinated by this glimpse into a secret world she never knew existed. People feared Gypsies, and now she knew why. The *Gitano* lived life on the edge.

As soon as her life calmed down, she decided she would write an article—maybe a whole series of them—on what Gypsies were really like, and what life was like for Gypsies.

∞

A Gypsy girl with black hair halfway down her back swayed around the circle of men, eyeing each as she passed. She stopped before Jake and invited him to dance. Though the music was tempting, Jake shook his head. He felt uneasy and self-conscious dancing flamenco with Elizabeth there. He knew that upper-class Mexicans considered the dance vulgar. Though not Mexican, Elizabeth was certainly upper class. Much to his surprise, he found himself a little embarrassed.

The Gypsy girl, both hands propped on her hips, swayed closer. "You too good to dance flamenco with me, eh? I thought you were different, but you're like all the others." She turned to walk away.

Jake caught her wrist. "Wait. One of us dances flamenco very well, but it's not me." He pointed to Gus. "He'll show you off to your friends and make you proud. He's very good. Remember, he's half Gypsy himself."

"Really?"

"Really," Jake said while leading her over to Gus.

Eyes gleaming, Gus listened. Then with a wide grin he led his partner to the center of the clearing. He nodded to the guitar players.

The guitars struck again, and on the downbeat he spun her in close to him and danced the male counterpart with her. He also was a big man. Though his footwork in riding boots was not as nimble as some of the others there dancing, he still knew all the right moves. He slapped his hand, his thigh, his foot. The Gypsies shouted and clapped. Arms over his head, he snapped his fingers. Hammering his feet, he circled his partner.

The Gypsies looked stunned.

Jake laughed to himself. Elizabeth would never know he'd turned the dance down, not for himself, but for her. Funny, but for some reason, that woman brought out the best in him. He frowned and decided he had to think about that.

Gus finished to applause and approving shouts. No one dreamed a gringo Ranger would know flamenco. He and his Gypsy partner strolled off together.

∞

A Gypsy man pulled Elizabeth to her feet and led her into the circle. She attempted to dance flamenco in her boots and pants. She stamped her feet and burst out laughing. Everyone seemed to understand that she wore men's clothes to hide from the police, and they loved her for it.

Arms high in the air, long hair flying around her face, she called, "Hoopa hoopa hoopa!" and stamped her feet in time to the music. It didn't matter to her that she didn't know what she was doing. Jake doubled over with laughter. The Gypsies grinned and clapped with her.

Standing in a circle of women, she had another glass of wine. And another.

You've had more wine tonight than you've had in a year! she scolded herself.

And she felt muzzy from it.

She slipped away and sat on the ground near one of the caves the Gypsies used for shelter. Watching the dancers and enjoying the music, she leaned against the cool stone with a smile.

The thrumming of the guitars coaxed her eyelids lower and made her sleepy. A minute later, her eyes closed.

"I've had too much wine," she whispered.

"I think you're right," a deep voice said.

An arm she recognized reached around her back, another arm under her knees, and she was lifted. With a sigh she turned her face into a familiar shoulder.

∞

"Where do you want her bed sack?" Fred asked.

"Right there's fine, away from the door," Jake said. He hauled his own blankets across the floor, just inside the front of the tent.

Fred spread Elizabeth's bed sack on the sole mattress in the tent, where Jake laid her down. In the light of a flickering oil lamp, he pulled off her boots and socks. Emotion welled up inside him, tugged at him. She was exhausted and she'd had too much wine.

"Gus will be late coming back," he said to Fred. "I'll stay with her for now, maybe get some sleep myself."

Fred nodded. "I think we'll be all right here. Place seems safe. Lots of people." With that, he said good night, turned, and left.

Jake tucked a blanket around her shoulders. Then he went and lay down near the front of the tent where he could keep watch for a while. He unlaced his boots and wrestled them off.

Settling back, his thoughts went immediately to Texas and Colonel Gordon's offer to come work with him. Tempting. It could put him on a fast promotion track to the rank of colonel.

He couldn't predict Elizabeth's reaction to that. It would be a huge step up for him.

But more and more, he found himself considering leaving the Rangers when his time was up and going into *real* law. The advantage would be living a more normal life, a life involved with politics and the public. No more chasing after outlaws.

Still, he couldn't figure her out. Or himself, for that matter. The signals were subtle, but nevertheless were there: the almost constant eye contact between them, the casual touching, on his part as well as hers. He knew—but he wasn't sure she did—that the classy Elizabeth Evans was as attracted to him as he was to her. The way she'd kissed him had given her away.

He shifted on the bed sack, looking at her in the dim light, the slight rising and falling of her form as she breathed. Though the ground was hard, he barely noticed it. Rangers were as used to sleeping on the ground as in a bed. But not Elizabeth, not a soft-skinned little woman. He was glad then she had a mattress on which to rest. He wanted only good dreams for her this night.

He rolled over so he could see the tent's door, yet his mind was still very much on her. He couldn't deny that she did something to him. Her smile, her voice, even the way she walked affected him. And deep inside, something rebelled at being so moved without knowing why.

A sigh blew out of him.

He suspected he *did* know why.

Deep down, a wariness stirred. He'd had it before, the warning all soldiers got going into battle when the odds were against them.

A frozen lake he'd started across as a boy flashed through his mind. He was out in the center before he realized the ice under his boots had moved, as if he were standing on loose marbles. His stomach turned to air. Mid-stride, he stopped and slowly, very slowly, backed up.

He knew then, as now, he could break through any minute and be in over his head with her.

If he wasn't already.

The tent lay in deep shadows, lit only by one small lantern. He rose up and walked over to her, gently pushed her hair aside with the back of his hand so he could see her better.

Her mouth was right there, only inches from his.

He suddenly wanted to kiss away every hurt she'd had in the last few days. He went down on one arm beside her. Barely touching her, he brushed his mouth lightly across hers, feeling her lips soften under his. They tasted faintly of wine.

"G'night," he whispered, then reached over and grabbed an extra blanket. He moved back to the far side of the tent. Staring into the dark, he lay on his bed and turned his back to her.

Even honor had its limits.

Twelve

IN SOME FAR, FOGGY PART OF HER BRAIN, Elizabeth vaguely realized someone was shaking her shoulder.

"Elizabeth, wake up. I've brought you coffee."

Her eyelids fluttered several times. Eyes closed, she drifted, floating in the dream shadows between sleeping and waking, aware only of Carl's hand on her shoulder. She snuggled closer against a solid hip and a hard leg that seemed somehow longer than she remembered. The first tenuous doubts tugged at her sleep. Not yet . . . not yet.

Kneeling on her bed sack, Carl shook her gently again. It had been so long. She stretched against him.

"Kiss me," she whispered sleepily.

"Not a good idea," said a male voice, not Carl's.

Elizabeth exploded from sleep. Wild-eyed, arms and legs flailing, she struggled to sit up, wriggling in thirteen different directions at once.

Hands faster than hers shot out, seized her wrists and clamped them together above her head. He threw a leg over her knees and pinned her to the blankets. The hard wall of his chest held her down with such strength it was useless to resist. She strained to free herself anyway.

"Jake, Jake!" She called him for help.

"Hey now, what's all this about? I'm right here," Jake said. His fingers tightened on her wrists.

She stared up at the stern mouth, at the jaw covered with pale stubble. As she twisted against the steel grip of his hands, her eyes slowly focused. Jake was already there.

"Stop squirming and wake up! You had too much wine last night and fell asleep outside. I put you to bed."

Her mouth fell open. "I had one glass of wine."

"I lost count at your third. And three glasses of that Gypsy wine would knock *me* flat."

Her eyes locked with his. "It did taste a little strong," she said slowly.

"Twice I tried to tell you, but you got snippy and told me to go away."

Way off in the back of her mind she also heard his smothered laugh when she told him to leave her alone and go find his lady friends.

"I thought you were just bossing me around."

He hid a smile. "When I boss you around, you'll know it."

She drew in a sharp breath.

He did the same. His jaw bunched, two hard knots in front of his ears. "I don't know what you were thinking, but I slept over there." He pointed across the tent to the other pile of blankets.

Uncertain, she sat up straight. The man beside her was all scowls and muscle and completely dressed. And so was she. She frowned and looked up at him.

"Finally figured it out, did you?" he said with a tight smile.

Her face burned, and an empty feeling hollowed her stomach. He'd misunderstood her struggling.

"I'm not thinking anything. I was half asleep and dreaming about Carl, which I haven't done for years. I'm sorry you misunderstood."

"Forget it," he said.

"Thank you for looking after me last night. You must be getting tired of that." Her voice faltered, the words stuck in her throat.

He chuckled. "You're quite welcome." Jake shoved to his feet, then reached down and pulled her up alongside him.

"What happened last night was my fault, not yours. Maybe I shouldn't have stayed here with you, but one of us needed to watch you. Under the circumstances, any lady waking up like that would have reacted the way you did."

Now she felt guiltier than ever. Her head was splitting, and she felt like a fool. "I think I'm dying." Eyes closed, she massaged her temples.

He chuckled. "Your first hangover?"

"It's not funny."

"You were the cause of my first hangover. Apparently I'm the cause of yours. We're even now."

He handed her a steaming mug of coffee. She took one look at it and her stomach heaved. With a shudder she pushed the cup aside. "I can't drink that," she said.

"Got to—two cups at least."

She peeked through her fingers at the black coffee. The bitter aroma she normally loved made her stomach fish-flop. She shook her head.

He pushed the mug back in front of her. "*Now* I'm bossing you around."

"If you make me drink that, I'll probably throw up."

"If you don't drink it, you definitely will, and I'd rather you didn't do it in Laszlo's clean tent."

She glanced around. It *was* clean, everything made neat and tidy. Sourly she wished Jake were sloppy. But no. Mr. Perfect had folded the blankets and stacked their bedrolls near the door, ready to be loaded on the horses. Not a thing was out of place. Of course, there wasn't much to be out of place.

"Drink," he said.

She made a face, but did as he asked, telling herself if it didn't kill her first, it might help, and that drinking the coffee had absolutely nothing to do with the smile lurking in the back of his eyes. Fortunately the coffee tasted better than it smelled, and after a few swallows, her stomach settled down as if it, too, knew better than to buck this man. Even the headache seemed to ease. She drained the cup.

"More?" she groaned when he filled it again.

"Just one, and that should do it."

The sudden softness in his voice surprised her. Swallowing her protest, she sipped the coffee like medicine. It had been so long since a man fussed over her, she'd forgotten how it felt. She finished it and set the cup down.

She tried to smile back, but failed. With every right to be furious with her, he seemed almost amused and was trying to put *her* at ease. She took a deep breath and plowed on. "Chalk this morning up to my being a nervous widow."

"I already did," he said.

∞

Right after breakfast, Jake sat down with his hosts.

"We're getting ready to leave," he told Laszlo, and passed

him a few bills, apparently more money than Laszlo had seen in a long time. "I want you to know how to reach us if you need to." Jake wrote down how to contact him, either at Fort Bliss or the Rangers' Camp Annex.

Laszlo shook his head. "Until your group came, we had no friends in America. None. Now we have four, and three of them are Texas Rangers. I can hardly believe it. We had a little meeting after you went to bed last night and came up with a plan to get you home safely. We're going with you to the Rio Grande. Once you're across the river, you will be safe. But getting you there when they're looking for you—that's the problem." Then he looked up at a commotion outside and smiled. "I think our plan has arrived."

Six Gypsy vardos, ornately painted house wagons, rattled into the clearing and stopped in front of Laszlo's entrance. One vardo was driven by Gus, another by Fred, both pulled by horses with ribbons tied to their manes.

Laszlo and Jake stepped outside to observe. Fred's vardo was painted red and white with a purple door and windows, which had curtains. Behind them on horseback sat six men, two with guitars, one with a trumpet, and three women also on horses: Nadia, an older woman, and the girl Gus had flamencoed with.

Laszlo held up an embroidered white smock with long blousy sleeves. "I have one for each of you. Wear them over your clothes and pull your trousers out of your boots. Then you'll look more like us." He frowned at Jake. "Anyone can tell you're Rangers half a mile away—with those shirts, neckties, and knee-high riding boots."

Jake's eyebrows flew up when Elizabeth jumped down from Gus's vardo and twirled into Laszlo's kitchen. She looked like a different woman. She wore a blue and red polka-dot blouse, a white vest, and a gaudy flowered skirt. Her hair was wrapped in a gold scarf with long ends hanging down her front. She wore a long jangly necklace and gold hoop earrings the size of her fists. Jake couldn't take his eyes off her.

Laszlo slapped his thigh and laughed. "It's our Hoopa lady!"

Elizabeth went over and wrapped Jake's head in a black scarf to hide his hair, knotting it at the back of his neck. Jake swung up on his horse and fell in line with the others.

It was ten miles to the river crossing, and on the way they discussed how to handle any confrontations. They were, Laszlo had advised, on their way to a wedding in Juarez, and looking forward to one of their own soon. On two occasions, Laszlo delivered these words while laughing and nodding toward Jake and Elizabeth. The soldiers laughed and waved them on.

Twice, small patrols of Mexican troops rode by the plodding little caravan—singing, guitars playing. The trumpeter alerted everyone in advance when something out of the ordinary appeared.

Once, alerted by the trumpet playing "Here Comes the Bride," Jake and Elizabeth ducked inside the middle vardo. A large Mexican patrol with an officer rode alongside and motioned for them to stop.

The conversation outside grew louder and seemed to go on too long for Jake's comfort. When he heard footsteps coming up the wood steps to the vardo, Jake grabbed Elizabeth and sprawled into a chair. "Kiss me like you mean it," he said, pulling her onto his lap.

She threw her arms around his neck, and his lips met hers just before the door flew open.

The officer watched for a moment, then shouted out the door, "Head back to camp. It's not this one, either. Just a man and a woman, necking." He looked back over his shoulder at Jake and smiled.

∞

When they'd finally reached the Rio Grande, they stopped alongside the river and spread cloths on the grass as though for a picnic. As soon as the road was empty in both directions, they hugged, shook hands, and said their good-byes.

Quickly, Jake, Fred, and Gus collected their weapons, strapped on holsters and ammunition belts. Jake made a stirrup of his hands and boosted Elizabeth into the saddle. "Hurry up. Let's go. Now!" he called.

Without wasting a minute more, he led them down the riverbank and out into the water. Elizabeth followed him, her heart pounding.

She looked back across the river. The picnic cloths were gone, the bank completely empty now. It was as if they were never there. Following Jake's advice, the caravan had turned and was already heading up the road for the camp as she and the Rangers got themselves out into the river.

Close to the shore, the water was shallow. Now it was coming higher. With each step of the horse, it got deeper still.

When it rose to her horse's belly, she cried out, "Jake!"

He swung around. "It's all right. The horse doesn't want to drown, either. He'll swim when he has to. Just hold on tight and he'll get you to the other side. And keep talking to him, praising him."

"Good horsey, good horsey," she said, over and over again.

Jake stared at her, his shoulders shaking.

"Don't you laugh at me, Jake Nelson! I forgot my horse's name."

"I'm not laughing."

But he was grinning. *Cuss his hide.* Her back stiffened as she snatched back her tattered pride. She was a swimmer, and a good one. She just hoped her horse was, too.

She thumped the animal's neck the way Jake did his horse and held her feet out of the water.

∽

Elizabeth's horse scrambled up the bank on the other side.

"Yippee! Texas! I'm home, I'm home."

Jake was there at the river's edge, off his horse and waiting for her. He walked a few steps into the water and grabbed her horse's bridle. Nervous, the horse whinnied, stamping his feet, shaking off the water. Elizabeth squealed and held on tighter.

Jake laughed and fed her horse a lump of sugar, stroking his neck and calming him down. "Good job. Good boy." He gave him an affectionate scrub between the ears.

Gus and Fred rode up, their horses shaking themselves off, as well. "Nice work, Elizabeth," Gus said.

"Her horse was as nervous as she was coming across," Fred said to Jake. "Rolled his eyes the whole way over."

"So did she. Neither of them had ever done it before," Jake said.

"Jake! You didn't tell me that!" Elizabeth said.

"A good example of what *horse sense* is in people. It was better you didn't know."

"What if he had shaken me off in the river?"

"I was right alongside, if you remember. It helped him to see my 'bossy horse,' as you call him, swimming quietly."

Jake's horse grunted and nudged him forward with his head.

"Hey, Banjo, I didn't forget you," Jake said, and pulled out sugar for the other horses.

Elizabeth watched him climb into the saddle and start up the bank for the road.

Outside Ysleta, Texas, they took the Lower Road—the old army road—to El Paso and Fort Bliss. It was a dirt road, a potholed single lane and not nearly as good as the newer road built a few years ago, Jake said. But it was less traveled and a direct route to Fort Bliss. He didn't want to see anyone until after he'd spoken with Colonel Gordon and Senator Madison.

"We go right past the lane to your house," he said. "Let's stop in, take a look around, and get some clothes for you. I think it's best you come to the fort before deciding what to do."

Earlier, Jake had been strangely silent on the subject whenever she mentioned returning to the big house.

They turned through the gates and headed up the lane to Lloyd's house—her house now.

From the outside, the big white house was as pretty and as impressive as ever.

"When we were here last, the inside had been vandalized," Jake said. "Those Mexican soldiers did a lot of damage in a short time."

The Rangers swung off their horses and went up the steps to the porch.

∽

Standing in the doorway, Elizabeth stared at the living room. Her stomach sank. Broken glass lay everywhere, with lamps and pictures broken and furniture thrown about, their cushions split open. Sickened by the destruction, she went upstairs to her room, picked her clothes off the floor, and put them into a valise.

"A couple of outfits should be more than enough," she told Jake.

"You don't know how long you'll have to be at the fort. Better plan on coming back to get more." He grabbed the valise and carried it downstairs.

She frowned at his back as he walked out the door. *This* was her home, not the fort. She decided she wouldn't stay out there one day longer than she had to. She needed to talk to her father. He'd straighten Jake out.

Alone for the first time, she walked down the hall to Lloyd's room. Stepping inside, she hiccupped on a sob and leaned her forehead against the doorjamb. Hot tears filled her eyes.

She'd loved him for a hundred different reasons. She'd just turned six when their mother drowned on a picnic outing. Ten years older than Elizabeth, he'd helped their father raise his little sister. He'd taught her to fish in the Potomac and to swim, which their mother couldn't do. He'd dried her tears and fixed her dolls. He'd taught her how to waltz and how to sit like a lady.

What would she do without him?

She missed him already.

Thirteen

AT TWO THAT AFTERNOON, Jake saluted and stood before the desk of the battalion commander, Colonel Greg Gordon. A tall, slender man with thinning gray hair.

Gordon returned the salute and laughed. "Don't let Commander King see you do that," he said. "According to him, Rangers salute no one but God Almighty."

He waved Jake to a chair. "Speaking of whom, when's the last time you were inside a church?"

"Actually I've spent the last few days in one and even spent the night there. I left with the abbot's personal blessing." He laughed out loud at Gordon's surprised look. "We hid out in a monastery in the mountains in Chihuahua," he explained. "I know the abbot."

As a young lieutenant, Jake served under Gordon in the Fourth Cavalry until Gordon accepted a promotion. When Gordon was later assigned to Fort Bliss, Jake was pleased. He respected Gordon, as a man and as a commander.

Now, occasionally, Gordon trained with Jake's Rangers, doing five-mile runs in the morning with them every chance he got. Sometimes Jake found himself running alongside Gordon, who was glad to get out from behind his desk.

The colonel's aide knocked and stuck his head in. "Senator Madison's here, Colonel."

Colonel Gordon met him at the door. "Come in, Senator, and meet Captain Nelson. He just walked in himself. Have you seen your daughter yet?"

"A few minutes ago. I left her at my quarters with Ruthie," the senator said. "They were down on the floor hugging and playing jacks when I left."

He looked over at Jake. "And I've heard a lot about you. I understand you don't think much of her going back to live alone in a big empty vandalized house a few miles from the Mexican border."

"That's right, sir. Not without security, and not until we see what's going to happen in Mexico. In fact, I'd like her under twenty-four-hour guard."

"You figured this situation out fast. I agree completely. Thank you for that. And thank you for bringing my daughter back safely. She's all I have." He cleared his throat.

Colonel Gordon spoke up. "I've already offered the senator's quarters here on base for Elizabeth," he said to Jake. "On the post, she's certainly safe. Ruthie can stay with our family and go to the nursery school with my four-year-old when Elizabeth's not there." He smiled. "That's one of the privileges of being a Texas senator's daughter at a Texas Army post."

Jake sat and talked with the men for a moment, telling them how they'd gotten out of Mexico. "We need to spend a couple of hours together. I haven't had a chance to fill Colonel Gordon in on what all took place last week. Everything points to General Diego's growing revolt. I think he intended to use Lloyd's death to force the U.S.

into reacting. Now he may be trying to raise the stakes. If so, we may have a problem. Elizabeth could be in real danger."

Senator Madison walked to the window. "I was afraid of that. You think they'd abduct her again?" he asked.

Jake studied the floor, thinking before he answered. "I don't know. It would be easier and safer for them not to."

"Just kill her, you mean."

Jake shook his head. "I'm thinking worst cases, you know. The reason against it is their desire that Washington know Mexicans did it. Abduction first, with a ransom note, would do that."

"I've been in touch with Washington and Austin. Both of them are watching this situation in Mexico. Both are very interested in your report." He turned around and smiled at Jake. "How about dinner tonight—you, me, and Elizabeth? You too, Greg, if you can get away."

The colonel shook his head. "Not tonight. My wife has invited friends for dinner at our home," he said.

"Captain, are you available?" Senator Madison asked.

"With pleasure, sir. What time? I have a buggy and can pick up you and Elizabeth."

"Seven o'clock sounds fine." Gordon looked up. "But you haven't checked in with your own office, Jake. Go do what you have to on that end. We'll talk in the morning, probably all morning. The adjutant general is coming up from Austin."

Jake shook the senator's hand. "I'll pick you up at seven. A real pleasure to meet you, Senator."

Senator Madison watched him leave and shook his head. "Where did you find him?"

"I didn't," Colonel Gordon said. "He found me. Ten years ago, I was his commander at Fort Dodge and managed to get myself shot in an Apache raid. Jake was a kid lieutenant and rode out on the field to find me. He rides like an Indian, hanging on the far side of his horse. He kept that horse between us and the bullets and dragged me out of there while I still had my hair."

"Sounds like we both owe him," Senator Madison said quietly.

"I'm trying to get him to rejoin the Cavalry and come work with me," Colonel Gordon said. "I'm looking for a new Executive Officer to head things up." Gordon closed a folder on his desk and leaned back in his chair.

"Which puts him in line to take over the battalion when you leave."

Colonel Gordon nodded. "He's ready. Texas Rangers have a certain professionalism about them, as well as a certain stubbornness. Nelson has both. For him, there is one way— the Ranger way. If a door is locked, kick it open. Jake Nelson is a door-kicker." Gordon chuckled. "And I understand you've got a front door to prove it."

Madison's eyebrows went up. "So that's what happened. Glad he did it. He got my granddaughter out alive."

The senator stood and returned to the window. "They didn't know what they might find in that house. I think they expected to find everyone killed." Staring out the window, he covered his eyes briefly and said, "I know I did. That was the worst train ride of my life."

Fourteen

JAKE LEFT COLONEL GORDON'S OFFICE and hurried down the stairs of the adobe-and-wood headquarters building. At the hitching rail, he untied his horse and swung himself into the saddle. As he did, his eyes fastened on the steeple of the white adobe chapel on the other side of the parade grounds. At the chaplain's request to the fort's commander, the steeple did not have a cross on top so the building could serve as a place of prayer for both non-Christians as well as Christians. Jake made a squeaking sound with his lips and trotted around the manicured grounds, heading toward the chapel.

Quickly he tied Banjo to another rail, took the front steps two at a time, and knocked on the office door. A small brass plate read *Major William Tyler, Chaplain*, and under that, *God Is Everywhere*.

Jake and Bill Tyler had known each other for years, going back to when they were both part of the Fourth Cavalry. Tyler, an ordained minister, graduated from Chicago Divinity School. He was a career military chaplain, and Jake trusted him completely.

"Jake, hello! Come in, come in. Heard about that Mexican operation of yours and was worried. When did you get back?"

"This morning." Jake smiled and grabbed his hand. "Got a minute, Reverend?" He tossed his hat on a nearby table.

"For you, always." Tyler waved Jake to a chair in the office, then slid his desk chair over and sat facing him. "What's on your mind?" he asked.

Jake's thoughts churned, trying to figure the best way to bring this up. He didn't want to sound too serious, but Tyler was nobody's fool. He would have it—and Jake—diagnosed in a minute.

Jake took a deep breath and started talking. "It's about a woman I just met. Nine days ago, to be exact." He went on to tell Tyler about this woman, about her being a widow, and the ring that still remained on her finger.

"Why would a woman who's been a widow for three years still wear her wedding ring?" Jake asked.

"Probably to keep men away, to give the appearance of being married. Most men stay away from a married woman. My sister wore hers after her husband died. Women are terribly vulnerable when they lose a husband. More so than us, I suspect. It's a hard thing for anyone to get over. Is she seeing other men?"

Jake ran a hand through his hair. He got up and walked to Tyler's desk and leaned against it. "I gathered from her conversation she isn't. Not at all."

"I'm not surprised. If she were seeing other men, the ring would be long gone. You can give a sigh of relief and relax. She just hasn't met the man yet to replace her dead husband."

"Or maybe she still loves him," Jake said.

Tyler was quiet for a moment, then shook his head slowly. "Whether she does or not, when the right guy comes into her life now, that ring will fly off her finger. But wearing it now says a lot of good things about her."

One corner of Jake's mouth dug in deep.

"Who is this woman?"

"Elizabeth Evans. Senator Madison's daughter."

Tyler let out a soft whistle. "The one you went to Mexico after?"

Jake nodded.

"I've heard about her. Beautiful girl, they say." He sighed. "I liked her brother Lloyd. Sad day. I gave the benediction at his funeral."

"I liked him too—he was a good man."

"So, if I'm reading this right, you sound interested in Elizabeth."

"I could be."

Tyler smiled. "It's about time. That business with Audrey was ugly, but it worked out well for you because she wasn't up to being an officer's wife. Those of us who knew you and knew her were afraid she'd hold you back. You must have been badly stung by it, because you've stayed away from women since then."

"I guess I did for a while."

"A long while."

Jake checked his watch and pushed off the desk. "Thanks, Bill. I feel better for talking to you. I'll just shut up and wait until she's ready. For now, I have to leave. I'm taking Elizabeth to dinner tonight."

Tyler stood and handed Jake his hat. "One last thing. The

ring business tells me you should handle this lady with kid gloves. If you really like her, take it slow. Be gentle, and sweet. Forget you're a big, bad Texas Ranger. Don't intimidate her."

Jake gave a quiet snort. "Are you kidding? She's half my size and she intimidates *me*."

Tyler threw his head back and burst out laughing. "Thank God. I haven't met her yet, and I love her already!"

∽

Jake spurred his horse into an easy gallop and took the trail from Fort Bliss to the Annex, wondering what he'd find when he got to his office.

"Hello, Murphy," he said to his clerk. "Got any good news for me?"

"Hello yourself, Captain. Glad to see you're back in one piece."

"So am I, believe me. You never know in Mexico. Anything happen I should know about?"

"Couple things." Murphy gestured to a long, narrow wooden telephone hanging on the wall. "That came in handy. They had a jailbreak down in Ysleta last week. Prisoner took off through the back country. We got the call from Ysleta and rode out fifteen minutes later. By nightfall we had him. Report's on your desk. And this just came from the hospital." He handed a paper to Jake. "Private Hernandez is in the hospital with a busted leg and a busted arm. Horse threw him."

"In C Company, isn't he?"

Murphy nodded.

"He's a good rider. What happened?"

"Bear jumped his horse. The horse reared and pitched

Hernandez into a tree. He was hurt pretty bad, unconscious when they brought him in."

"Tell you what, Murphy. You go on, get out of here early for a change. On your way, stick your head in at C Company and ask Sergeant Greer to come fill me in."

"I'll do that right now, and thank you." Murphy swiftly cleared his desk, then passed Jake a handful of messages. "These came in while you were gone. There were more, of course, but Lieutenant Sanders handled them." He turned and started for the door.

"Wait, Murphy—what's the name of that store in El Paso where you got flowers for your mother?"

"Not really a store; it's part of the Fashion Saloon. They got electric lights in there, you know. Business is booming. Don't know where their liquor comes from, but they get fresh flowers in every day from the big cities." Murphy then left to catch Hernandez's sergeant.

Leafing through the messages Murphy had given him, Jake shook his head. While he was in Mexico, three problems had surfaced: Company B's capture of the escaped prisoner, a bar fight and shooting in El Paso, and a follow-up on twenty-five stolen cattle.

Company A was out on a scheduled patrol, and his own D Company was resting and getting fat.

He smiled. Tomorrow might be a great day for a five-mile run.

Hitching his leg up, he sat on a corner of his desk. He reached for the foot-high stack of reports and read the top one. He had just finished reading it when Sergeant Greer of C Company stepped into the office to fill him in on Private Hernandez.

Jake made notes: facts, figures, dates, impersonal information necessary for him to recommend keeping Hernandez in the Rangers or to let him go.

But Hernandez the Ranger jumped off the page when Sergeant Greer said the young private burst into tears when told he might be discharged.

That had some uncomfortable similarities for Jake, who'd spent weeks in a wheeled chair with a shot-up hip and worried about the same thing—his Army career ending because, like Hernandez, he hadn't known what was behind him, either. For Jake, it was an Apache with a loaded Winchester.

Jake checked his pocket watch. If he hurried, he had time to go see Hernandez before dinnertime.

∞

Jake ran up the stairs to the third floor of the hospital building. According to his sergeant, Jim Hernandez was recovering in Room 310.

"Hi, Marge," Jake said to the gray-haired nurse he'd seen many times before. He looked at the pale face of his youngest Ranger lying in a bed by the window. His leg was elevated by a pulley and wires attached to a metal frame above the bed.

Jake pulled up a chair. "How's the leg, Jim?"

"I'll be all right, Captain. Just may take a little time is all."

"Sergeant Greer and I talked this afternoon, and both of us want you to stay with the Rangers—if that's what you want. You told me last month you planned on reenlisting when your time is up. You still feel that way?"

Jim nodded, his eyes filling with tears. "I was afraid you'd kick me out because of this." He gestured with his good arm at his leg in a cast.

"We'll find you a job you can do sitting down. A couple of months and you'll be back in your saddle. Just do what Marge tells you. Right, Marge?"

"That's right, Captain," Marge said while looking at Jim.

Jake stood and patted Jim's shoulder. "Get well now. If you need anything, tell Marge and she'll let me know. I'll check back in a day or so."

Marge walked him to the door. "Thank you for stopping in," she said. "That's the first time I've seen that boy smile since he got here."

Fifteen

Fort Bliss Emergency Room

"ELIZABETH! YOU'RE BACK!" The dark-haired nurse rushed around the end of the desk and hugged her hard. "I heard this morning you were back. The Rangers aren't saying a word, but the rest of this fort has been buzzing for a week. It was supposed to be a big secret, but everyone knew. How are you?"

Elizabeth returned Suzanne Peterson's hug. Suzanne lived on post with her parents. Her father was a major. She and Suzanne had met when Elizabeth came out to visit Lloyd two years earlier.

"I wanted to stop in and say hello before I go home and take a nap," Elizabeth said. "I'm staying with my dad on post. I've been talking all morning to military people and I'm tired."

Suzanne returned to her station behind the desk and picked up a chart listing new patients. "I'm so sorry about your brother. Everyone in town was at the funeral."

"Thank you . . . to be honest, it hasn't sunk in yet."

Suzanne nodded. "By the way, your housekeeper brought Ruthie in for a doctor to see her—the same day they took you. Captain Nelson ordered it."

"I'm not surprised he sent Ruthie to the doctor," Elizabeth said. "He's sweet."

"He may be a lot of things, but I wouldn't call him *sweet*."

Elizabeth chuckled. "Funny, he said the same thing."

"Jake Nelson is a hard-nosed Ranger officer. From what I hear, he's never served a day in anything but combat units."

"I thought that at first too, but I was wrong about him. He isn't hard-nosed at all. He's considerate and kind."

Suzanne snorted. "Considerate and kind? A Texas Ranger? Well, don't tell anyone. You'll ruin his image."

"Dad is taking us to dinner tonight at the Grand Hotel. The three of us wanted to get away from the fort and eat someplace nice, someplace with music."

The outside door to the Emergency Room opened. "Afternoon, ladies. I'm looking for Miz Elizabeth Evans."

"That's me," Elizabeth said, turning around.

"Fashion Florist, ma'am. Delivery for you."

He handed her a large bundle of green tissue paper swathed around some kind of flowers.

Smiling, Elizabeth laid them on the counter and fished down through all the paper. "Oh, look, Suzanne! Roses! They're beautiful."

"Who sent them?" Suzanne asked.

"My father, I'm sure." As she plucked out the small card nestled in among the tissue paper, her jaw dropped.

"Well?" Suzanne said.

Shaking her head, she leaned over the counter and passed

the card to Suzanne. "I can't believe he did this," Elizabeth said.

" 'Welcome home. I'm still smiling. Jake,' " Suzanne read aloud. "Well, you must be right. You said he was sweet. What's he smiling about?"

"I wish I knew."

Hands on her hips, Suzanne looked across the desk. "Is there something you're not telling me here?" She read the card again. "Still smiling, is he? Frankly I didn't think that man knew *how* to smile."

"What are you talking about? He smiles all the time."

"With you maybe, not with anyone else. He's tough, and it shows. He's a straight shooter. Leave it to you to find one. He's right out of the old officer mold—never do anything to shame the uniform. I think he's also got your number. You must have knocked him off his feet, and now he intends to knock you off yours."

Elizabeth gestured to the flowers. "I never know what to expect from him. To tell you the truth, I don't understand him at all."

"Did he ever tell you how he got that scar on his hip?" Suzanne asked.

Elizabeth stiffened. "Of course not. I didn't know he had a scar there."

"Well, he does. I saw it last year when they had him on the examining table to be checked. That scar is as big as your hand. It's a wonder the man can even walk, let alone shoot everything that moves and blow things up."

"Oh, be serious."

"I'm dead serious. That's what Texas Rangers do. For starters. After that, they can get ugly."

"I'm not sure any of them are like that, and certainly not Jake. He's different."

"Not to mention aggressive and determined."

Elizabeth laughed. "You left out intelligent and handsome."

"Didn't think you noticed such things."

"I noticed."

Apparently, however, she was a relic from the last century. Sunday school teaching and church had shaped her values. And Lloyd's, too.

Suzanne's features softened. "Have fun tonight. All kidding aside, I think it's great you've changed your mind about men in the military."

Elizabeth gathered up the green bundle of flowers. "I'd better get these in water."

"There's water in the staff room around the corner. You might even find a vase in the cupboard."

As Elizabeth headed for the hallway to the staff room, she called back over her shoulder, "And I have not changed my mind."

"Oh yes, you have," Suzanne said quietly.

⚭

Between arranging them and looking at them and wondering why he sent them, the roses were making her crazy. Nibbling on her lower lip, Elizabeth slipped the last long stem into the vase she'd found in the staff room. She cocked her head, removed a bud, and put it on the left side this time. Perfect. She buried her face in the pretty red petals and smiled, ridiculously pleased.

Picking up the vase, she left the staff room, humming

under her breath. Even the dingy green walls of this place looked sunny and fresh today.

Walking toward her, rattling a food cart ahead of him, was an orderly. Elizabeth waved and grinned, and realized she'd been doing that a lot lately.

∽

Head on, Jake Nelson was even bigger than she remembered, an imposingly tall man with wide shoulders and a neck as big around as her thigh. In a light tan corduroy jacket and dark brown trousers, Jake took up the whole doorway. Arms folded, he leaned against the doorframe.

"Hello," she said, smiling.

Jake took off a hat the same color as his jacket and stepped past her into her father's temporary quarters at Fort Bliss.

From the pearl stud earrings she wore, to the trim linen dress and high-heeled sandals, he seemed to be analyzing her, cataloging her. His eyelids drooped sleepily as his gaze settled on her figure.

She'd dressed carefully for tonight. Before deciding on the lavender linen dress, she pulled one outfit after another out of the valise and held them up in front of the mirror. From the look on Jake's face, she'd made the right choice.

"Thank you for the flowers," she said, indicating the vase of red roses on the coffee table. "They are so beautiful."

He smiled. "You mean boo-ful, like you," he said softly.

Her cheeks warmed. *Quit it*, she told herself. Twenty-three-year-old widows do not blush. "As soon as I get my reticule, I'm ready to go." Hoping her face wasn't as red as the flowers, she reached for the small beaded reticule open on a nearby table. When she picked it up, it slipped from her hand. Coin purse, comb, perfume, and pencil spilled to the floor. Her perfume rolled under a chair.

She stooped to pick them up.

Jake went down on one knee and felt around under the chair for the perfume. His fingers brushed hers. She snatched her hand away as if he'd touched her with a lit match.

"Darlin'," he said, rising to his feet, "do I make you nervous or something?"

Towering over her—a big, intimidating Ranger officer—he most certainly did.

"Of course not," she lied. "After last week, we're practically old friends." Old friends. Not a good choice of words. She flushed, hoping he wasn't remembering the kisses.

She threw everything back into the reticule. She pulled the drawstring closed and looked up. "Ready to go?"

"Whoa there. Not so fast. Where's your father? I've been looking forward all day to talking with him tonight." Jake looked up, as if expecting the senator to step out of the kitchen.

"I'm sorry, Jake, but Dad had to leave. He sent a message an hour ago that he was taking the six-fifteen evening train to Austin. Something came up with the adjutant general, he said. He'll be back in a couple of days. We'll make it up when he returns. He's looking forward to talking with you."

Jake led her out to the buggy and helped her in.

Elizabeth settled herself comfortably into the soft leather seat and watched him take charge. He drove the buggy and horse with intense concentration, his eyes rarely leaving the road except to dart quick glances around, as if he needed to know where everything was all the time. Typical Ranger.

Or maybe typical Reconnaissance. He used to be a scout, after all—considered the most trusted and reliable members of the Armed Forces. They were the nameless men who slipped deep inside enemy lines and did whatever they'd been sent to do. And then got themselves out, usually without a trace.

That troubled her.

Jake glanced at her. "I heard you playing the piano the other day at the orphanage," he said. "You're very good. I didn't know you could play like that. And your favorite composer would be . . . ?"

"Chopin for the piano, of course. I like others also, especially Vivaldi for strings. He's an old one, but he's wonderful. Some of his pieces nearly make me cry." She turned in her seat. "Carl used to laugh at me for reacting to music like that."

Jake brushed aside a flare of annoyance.

Carl this. And Carl that.

His fingers tightened on the reins.

He couldn't care less what kind of music Carl Evans had liked. Jake guided the buggy into the center of the road, away from the ruts, and searched for something else to talk about other than her dead husband.

Forget Carl Evans.

Bad idea. Evans was part of her past, part of her. Not talking about him would be a mistake. Jake had been in the Cavalry, and he knew better. Knowing your enemy was half the battle.

"Tell me about Carl," he said. His voice had a tight, tucked-in sound that surprised him.

"What do you want to know?"

Everything. "What was he like?" he asked smoothly, then steeled himself for the answer.

"Wonderful. Always in a good mood." The answer bubbled up. "One of those people who wake up in the morning whistling. Handsome, smart. Everybody liked him."

So how do I make you forget him?

"He was a towhead, like you."

Jake nodded. "You told me." *Twice.*

She gazed out the window for a moment, then turned and looked at him, the dimple in her cheek lighting her face. "In some ways, you remind me of him."

His stomach knotted. That was the *last* thing he wanted to hear.

"Too bad you and Carl never met. I think you two would have gotten on well."

Not likely. They were both Cavalry. They would've fought over her like two stallions. Truth was, if he'd known her before she married Evans, he would have done everything he could to steal her from him. And one way or another, he would have.

He slid her another glance and smiled to himself.

He was still going to.

Sixteen

HE THREADED THEIR BUGGY in ahead of two others stopped in front of the Grand Hotel. The hotel took up nearly the whole block, rising four stories, the tallest building in El Paso. As soon as they stopped, an attendant stepped up, opened Elizabeth's door, and helped her down to the sidewalk.

Jake exited his side, and another attendant drove the buggy off to the Grand's own livery for their customers. Jake walked around to meet Elizabeth.

The Grand was the most luxurious hotel this side of San Antonio. He'd been here several times, the last time with Lloyd Madison the evening before they left to meet Ricardo Romero in Mexico. It had quietly elegant dining rooms, a dance floor, and a broad open promenade for walking along the riverside.

Following her into the hotel, Jake studied the dark-haired lady in lavender linen and high-heeled sandals rustling ahead of him. She'd caught her dark hair into thick braids coiled over each ear. Beautiful. He liked her hair like that.

Back straight, skirt swinging, Elizabeth ascended the carpeted stairway to the restaurant deck.

Beautiful little back.
Beautiful little everything.

Upstairs, he noticed other men turn their heads, sneaking glances at her as the steward escorted them to their table. In one way, that pleased him. In another, it did not.

He cupped her elbow possessively and guided her across the dining room. "Watch your step—the floor's uneven," he said. It wasn't. It was dead level.

Models of sailing ships hung on the walls. Their table was in a private corner with a heavy-looking brass porthole overlooking the Rio Grande. A blood-red sunset lit up the sky. Even the river looked rosy.

Elizabeth turned from the window back to Jake and the low hum of voices around them. "This is delightful, as nice as any place in Washington," she said. "This town is growing so fast. I can hardly wait to get started with the paper."

She sounded confident, positive, a woman who knew what she wanted. Or didn't want. And at the moment, he suspected, what she didn't want was him. Eyes narrowed, Jake leaned back in his chair. She was a challenge, all right.

For his twelfth birthday, his stepfather had given him a horse of his own, a wild young filly no one could get near. She'd tossed her head and bucked him off every time he got in the saddle. Bruised and sore, his wrist in a cast—she'd also kicked him—he kept climbing onto her back. It took him a month of chasing and yelling at her, but one day she'd finally let him sit on her.

Jake studied the pretty dark-haired woman across the table and made small, damp rings on the tablecloth with his water glass. His mind turned, making comparisons.

Elizabeth was a little like that filly—arching her neck and rolling her eyes and running away from him.

Easy girl. Easy now. Mentally he picked up a rope and halter and started after her.

A minute later, he set his glass down and looked over. "Do you have any other brothers or sisters?"

She shook her head. "Lloyd was my only brother. How about you?"

He eased his breath out. About time she showed some interest in him. "No brothers or sisters. My stepfather had a small herd of milk cows and sold to the townspeople."

Masculine Texas charm oozed from every pore, smooth as banana cream. No pressure on the lady, but no escape, either. Elizabeth set the topic of conversation, and Jake picked up on it. Just knowing what he was doing and why gave him an advantage he didn't hesitate to use.

He entertained her, kept her amused, drawling one funny little tale after another.

When he was five years old, he told her, he dropped caterpillars down a neighbor girl's pinafore, and his mother spanked him. At nine, he threw eggs at the preacher's dog when it growled at him, and his mother spanked him again.

As a boy growing up, he was on the small side. Because he read better than even the older boys, they singled him out to pick on. He started carrying a garter snake in his pocket. At the first sign of trouble from one of the older boys, he yanked his snake out and dangled it in the bully's face. The yellow-striped snake, whipping back and forth in the air, had its mouth wide open and snapping—all worked up from being carried around in Jake's pocket all day. The bigger boys left Jake and his crawly friend alone.

Elizabeth broke out laughing and leaned forward. A delightful laugh, soft and throaty. She should do that more often. Relieved, he watched her unwind, realizing she was also drawing *him* out. The back of his neck warmed. He hadn't revealed himself like this to a woman in years.

"Why did you join the Army?" she asked.

He wondered when she'd get around to that. "I joined mainly to get away from home. When I was fifteen I told my stepfather I wanted to go to college. He threw me up against the house, a regular occurrence with him. Said I didn't need more education to milk cows. I ran away that night and joined the Army the next day."

What Jake didn't tell her was what followed a few weeks later. During barracks inspection one day, they found a copy of Tolstoy's *War and Peace* hidden beneath his shirts. The sergeant confiscated the book.

A week later, they hit him with a bunch of tests. A month after that, they called him in to ask him if he would like to go to Officers' Training School.

Jake said he would, glad for the opportunity.

It was hard. He was younger than everyone else at the school but had been warned to keep quiet about it. The instructors were tough and so were the courses. He studied far into the night. When he graduated, he'd lost twenty pounds and was in the worst physical shape of his life. But it was the best thing he ever did for his Army career. Officer training taught him things about responsibility for others and leadership, about himself as a man that changed him forever.

"You could have been out long ago," Elizabeth said. "Why did you stay in?"

He composed his thoughts before he answered. The truth was that, for him, the Army was fun. And somewhere along the line, he discovered how much he loved his country. When parade drums rolled and the flag went by, he still got chills. He gazed across the table at Elizabeth and hid a smile.

Tell her that, and she'll run for the nearest door.

Instead, he hung his arm casually across the chair beside him and gave her a safe answer. "Staying in the Army keeps me out of the dairy business."

The waiter came and took their order from a French menu—a grilled salmon for him, a shrimp Newburg for her.

"And Chardonnay for madame," he finished in French, smiling. "I'll pass on the wine, *merci.*"

She glanced up. "You speak French?"

"No more than necessary. The Army sent me to school."

∞

Elizabeth recited to herself all the good, sound reasons for avoiding men like Jake. While it wasn't the Army, Rangers were quasi-military, and the work just as dangerous.

In spite of that, Captain Jake Nelson was fun to be with. He could always make her laugh, even in Mexico when she was under great stress.

And then the roses today. *"Boo-ful, like you,"* he'd said. Her cheeks heated just thinking about it. She hugged the words in her mind and looked down at her wine. It had been a long time since any man told her she was beautiful. A man didn't do that unless he was interested. She took a long sip of her wine and considered the possibility that for the first time in a long time, *she* was interested. But a Ranger officer?

She sighed.

Unfortunately, yes.

She closed both hands around her glass, tightly. A shudder chased through her. This gray-eyed, slow-talking man did crazy things to her insides. He was making her question everything she'd told herself about men the last three years.

This must not happen.

He was too much like Carl.

She finished her wine in silence and gazed at Jake's face. He had a square jaw with a deeply cleft chin. She could almost imagine her fingernail tracing the tiny trench, probing it.

Heat slid down her neck. *What is* wrong *with me?*

She blinked across at the man with the cute chin and cleared her throat.

Smiling, she set her glass down. "I went to the hospital today to see a nurse friend, and on the way I ran into one of our writers at the paper. I'd met him two years before but didn't recognize him. Fortunately, his memory was better than mine, and he stopped me to say hello. He's doing a piece on military food and taking a survey out at the fort of the foods soldiers like best."

Jake broke off a piece of roll and buttered it.

She glanced at the man in the tan corduroy jacket. He had the expression of a man who knew where he was going.

Despite the nice manners, he looked tough. She couldn't quite tell why, but perhaps it was the way he wore his hair, a little long, curling at the back of his neck.

Her gaze slipped to the fingers buttering the roll. His fingers were rather graceful for a man. Golden blond hairs curled from the shirt cuffs under the jacket and dusted the backs of his hands. His nails, she noted, were cut short, dull and natural looking. She hated shiny fingernails on men.

"I told him I'd talk to you about military food. It'll be good publicity for the fort. He's already interviewed two Fort Bliss cooks," she said.

"Glad to help. What do you need from me?"

"A few of your favorites. What do Rangers like to eat?"

"Depends on what they're doing. Riding for hours is physically draining. If they have to cook outside, our cooks use a lot of sausage, bacon, chops—things that cook fast and are filling. Rice, potatoes, and always end the meal with something sweet."

"Sounds like they're treated pretty well."

"Ranging and soldiering are hard work, and also lonely."

"And dangerous," she added.

"Sometimes. It's pretty boring a lot of the time. Which is why food is important. Cooks know that. The Army and the Rangers are family to their men, and family takes care of its own."

She busied herself with her shrimp, then looked up, her fork poised. "I don't know as I believe George—the writer doing the story—but he said a cook at the fort told him hungry Rangers will eat anything. Cooked or raw. Alive or dead." She leaned forward and lowered her voice. "He said Rangers even eat snakes."

∞

Jake's bite of roll went down the wrong way and he started to cough. He scooped up his glass of water to wash it down, his mind racing, trying to come up with something that wouldn't turn the ladylike Elizabeth's stomach, something not exactly the truth, but not exactly a lie, either.

"It's the civilized habits we have to get over. When a man is starving to death, he *will* eat anything," he said.

He'd taught every one of his Rangers how to stay alive in Texas. On one miserable desert operation, they'd eaten everything they had with them and gone three days with only what they could find to eat—roots and berries. On the third morning, light-headed with hunger, he'd seized the tail of a six-foot rattlesnake and yanked it from under a log. Five half-starved young men with knives fell on it. Twenty minutes later, that snake was skinned and sizzling over a cook fire.

He covered his mouth, struggling to keep a straight face, and looked across at Elizabeth.

Laughing, Elizabeth said, "So you *do* eat snakes!" The skin wrinkled on the bridge of her nose. "That's disgusting."

Jake nodded, wiped at his eyes. "Some people think it tastes a lot like chicken."

"Does it?"

He shook his head. "Tastes like snake to me."

With a smile, she leaned back in her chair and asked, "Can I quote you on that?"

∞

Over dessert, he listened to her with only one ear. The other listened to the music coming from the bar in the other room—guitars, piano, flute, the soft brush of drums, and the breathy groan of a new horn called a sax-o-phone. For two more songs he debated about asking her to dance.

A picture flashed in his head of her, warm and resting in

his arms at the Gypsy camp. The image was too powerful. He rose to his feet. Ignoring her startled expression, he pulled her out of her chair.

"Let's dance."

"I haven't danced in years," she said.

Gripping her hand, he led her onto the dance floor.

The pianist lowered his hands over the keyboard, and the music started again. Hand around her waist, Jake swung her against him in time with the music. He glided her backward, acutely aware of the woman in his arms.

They made a handsome couple, he thought, as they danced by a wall mirror. He was struck by how pretty she was with her head tipped back looking up at him. He couldn't stop smiling.

When the song ended, they stood on the dance floor with the other couples, clapping politely. The subtle fragrance she wore wafted around him. He took a deep breath and filled his lungs with the essence of her. It distracted him. *She* distracted him with that intriguing blend of brains and beauty.

Drums rolled and the band began to play a sentimental old song. He slid his arm around her waist again and pulled her against him. This time she rested her cheek against his chest. He wasn't imagining it. With each dance she was melting a little more into him.

Then came the guilt. He felt as if he was taking advantage of her, and he didn't mean to. When the music stopped, he led her toward the stairway that led down to the promenade. "Let's go outside," he said.

∞

A breeze fluttered the hem of Elizabeth's dress as they strolled together along the promenade. Jake's hand felt warm and solid, his fingers curved around hers. She glanced over at him. It had been so long since she'd truly enjoyed being with a man. In spite of what he did for a living, she liked this man.

The only ones on the promenade, they walked to the far end and leaned on the railing, gazing out over the river. Light from the restaurant spilled onto the water. Luminous and reflective, the river's mirrored surface lapped against the boardwalk.

Neither spoke, listening to the quiet shushing of water around them. Music floated out from the bar.

Jake turned her hand over in both of his. "Glad you came?"

"Very." The corners of her mouth curved.

His hand slipped to her waist, turned her toward him. He crooked her chin up and made her look at him.

When his gaze slipped to her mouth, she knew with absolute certainty she was about to be kissed.

Jake drew her up onto her toes. She clutched his shoulders in surprise at finding herself in his arms this way. Thoughts tumbled in her head. One part of her wanted to run away. Another part rooted her to the boardwalk. Don't be ridiculous, she thought, as his face lowered. One kiss wouldn't matter. In fact, she'd liked the other. . . .

A warm mouth covered hers. Even as she told herself not to, she closed her eyes. For just an instant, Carl's face blurred across her mind, then faded, obliterated by this man's lips.

Cradling the back of her head, he made a thick, pleased sound in his throat. He had a wonderful mouth, taking and giving at the same time, totally sure of himself. At that moment she felt the first small splinter in the hard shell she'd built around her emotions. Time slowed to a crawl as his lips moved over hers.

When he raised his face, she rested her forehead against his necktie. This man can *kiss*.

"I promised myself I wouldn't kiss you tonight," he said.

Twice she swallowed before she trusted herself to speak. "When did you mean to kiss me?"

"I don't know. I wanted to give you time to get used to me. I didn't want to rush you, but I guess I did."

His lips found hers again. Never breaking the kiss, he took a step backward into the shadows. This time there was a dreamy closeness to their kiss. He was sweet and affectionate, things she'd never suspected he could be. With a small, quiet moan, she closed her eyes and kissed him back.

When he lifted his mouth and looked down at her, his eyes were full of questions.

"Who are you afraid of—yourself or me?" he asked.

"Myself, I guess. You see, I don't know how to deal with you."

Shaking his head, he said, "There must be some kind of protocol for this. It's just not civilized to tell you I wanted to kiss you before I even knew your name. That's a first for me."

"Uncivilized, but honest."

She caught a quick white smile in the dark as he ran the ball of his thumb over her lower lip. "I'm attracted to you, Elizabeth Evans, and I think it's mutual—something neither of us expected. Or wanted. Especially you. So, say yes to tomorrow and let's start to learn about each other." He brushed her hair back from her face. "Suppose I pick you up for breakfast, and then we'll go to . . . I don't know, how about the train station?"

Her eyebrows flew up. "The train station?"

"Someplace in broad daylight with people around. Maybe then you'll relax with me. Maybe I'll even relax with you." Though he said it casually, his Texas drawl came out thicker than usual, revealing that he was more bothered than he let on.

One corner of his mouth kicked up. "You see, I don't know how to deal with you, either."

That unexpected admission surprised her. For a man like Jake Nelson, that must have cost him. She steeled herself to say no, but deep inside, her resolve was weakening. He'd done so much for her.

"But not the train station," she said.

"Where, then?"

She nibbled at her lower lip, thinking. "How about something outside? I overheard Gus telling one of the soldiers from maintenance that he saw beavers building a dam on that creek behind the fort. He said that can mean flooding. Let's take a canoe and go check it out."

He laughed. "How about we walk the creek instead?"

"Canoeing is more fun, and maybe I can get a story out of it."

"You're already writing a story about cooks and army food; now you want to take on the Corps of Engineers. What's next?"

"The hospital."

He shook his head.

She tugged at his necktie and smiled. "Breakfast at my house, but not too early, and then we can go sailing. Or something close to it."

∞

After he dropped her off at her father's house in the Distinguished Guests section of Fort Bliss, Jake drove over to Camp Annex and his own place in the Officers' Quarters. Knowing he was too preoccupied to sleep, he took his time in the stable, unhitching the horse and rubbing him down.

Later, sitting at the table in his kitchen, Jake slammed his palm down and pushed to his feet. When he took Elizabeth home earlier, he'd walked her up the outside steps to the door and kissed her good night.

On the forehead.

Staring glumly into the wooden icebox, he grabbed a bottle of milk, poured himself a glass and drank it. He filled the glass again, took it back to the table, and sprawled into a chair.

His life had been as hard as Elizabeth's had been easy. He'd had to work for everything he got—even in the Army. But she grew up cradled in luxury and security, clubs and fancy schools.

And because of that, you're going to push her aside?

Idly he turned the glass around and around, making small, wet circles on the tabletop.

Behind him, he heard the front door open.

A minute later, Gus filled the doorway, pulling both Colts from their holsters. He slid them onto the counter by the wash-up sink. Loosening his tie, he came over to the table, pulled out a chair and sat, then said, "Quiet night in El Paso. A purse snatching and a couple of gang kids spoiling for a fight. I chased them back across the river. How come you're still up?"

"I'm not sleepy," Jake said, rising as soon as Gus sat down.

"Don't want to talk to me, huh?"

"I'm not fit company for anybody tonight." Jake propped his foot on his chair and retied his boot.

"Where are you going?"

"Don't know. Maybe I'll walk awhile."

"Stay away from the fort, then," Gus said. "At this time of night, you'll get picked up in ten minutes." He reached a hand over and took Jake's arm. "Come on, sit back down. Who is she?"

Jake shot him a hard look. "What makes you think it's a girl?"

"I ran into Gino from the hotel's kitchen. He said you had a beautiful woman hanging all over you tonight. I figured that had to be our Elizabeth."

"It was. We danced, that's all, and she most certainly was not hanging all over me."

Of all the Annex Rangers, because he was the one in charge, he was the even-tempered one, the thoughtful, quiet one who never lost control. But just then, his tone had definitely become edgy.

"A no-fun evening, huh?" Gus said.

Jake shook his head. "I feel like I'm going downhill in a runaway wagon, and I've lost the brakes."

∞

Elizabeth kicked the sheet back. For the third night in a row, she couldn't get to sleep for thinking of Jake Nelson. This night—like the last two nights—she turned and tossed in bed. Every time she closed her eyes, she could feel his hands on her. She'd forgotten how good it felt, just to be held.

Staring at the ceiling, she remembered the solid feel of him in her arms, how strong his mouth had been on hers, how sweet it was to be kissed again. He made her feel like a woman. A pretty woman.

With a sigh, she stood and turned up the gas lamp on the night table and checked the clock. Three in the morning and she was wide awake.

She padded down the hall. In the quiet house, even her footsteps seemed loud to her ears. On her way through the living room, she picked up the vase of roses, carried it into the kitchen, and set it on the table.

She opened the icebox and poured herself a glass of tea from a pitcher, tasted it, and carried it over to the table.

She got a spoon from the drawer and added more sugar. Chin propped in her hands, she smiled at the flowers and stroked a fragile red bud about to open. It had been years since anyone sent her flowers.

A happy lightness rose inside her. She liked the man who had sent the flowers. A lot. She'd laughed more with Jake Nelson tonight than she had all year. He wasn't so serious with her as he was with the men. Instead, he'd teased and flirted with her, even danced with her.

And she had to admit: the attraction was mutual. The first time they'd kissed tonight had been like coming home after a long, long time away. Her reaction to him and his sweet, soft kiss surprised her.

In his arms, nothing else had mattered.

Absently she stirred her spoon in the tea, a small singing sound in the bottom of the glass. She licked the spoon and laid it aside, her thoughts crowding in on her.

For the first time since Carl died, she was interested in another man.

Uneasy, she rose from the chair and carried her glass to the sink, scolding herself. Common sense told her to stay away from him. Depending on where he was assigned and how many men he had under him, Rangers were gone much of the time. Though he wasn't U.S. Army, he was close, perhaps worse. The sleeping soldiers in Mexico flitted across her mind. What he was trained to do, what he would train others to do at the fort, was chilling to her. Flowers and a few kisses wouldn't change that.

Be sensible. Like Carl, all soldiers were trained to fight the enemy.

On the way back to bed, she stopped in front of the dresser. A different light-haired man looked out from a silver-framed photograph, a handsome young lieutenant smiling at the camera three years ago.

She picked up the photograph and ran her fingers across the cool glass. Carl could never call her name again or kiss her again or make her feel as Jake had done tonight. She smiled at the photograph, at her husband's frozen smile and unseeing eyes.

Hot tears welled. Standing by the dresser in the semidarkness of the room, she cried again for the loss of her Carl.

Their marriage had been too short. She'd had so much more love to give him than they were given time for. All her dreams of having his children and loving their grandchildren were lost, as well. And though a part of her would always love him, always belong to him, Carl was now a shadow, a memory.

It was time to move on.

"I'm so tired of being lonely," she whispered to his picture.

She set the frame back on the dresser and worked her wedding ring off, then slipped it and the photograph into the top drawer. For several moments she looked down at them.

Carl was yesterday.

Jake was today. Perhaps tomorrow.

Gently she closed the drawer.

Seventeen

"JUST A MINUTE!" Elizabeth wound a towel around her head and hurried to answer the doorbell. On her way, she glanced out the living room window.

A big-eared Army mule hitched to a green flatbed wagon was parked in front of the house.

She hesitated, then opened the door.

Jake stood on the porch, holding a paper bag from the bakery at Fort Bliss. He wore black trousers and a black shirt that clung like a second skin. And no riding boots.

"Am I late?" he asked innocently.

"You're an hour early, and you know it." She stepped aside and cinched the robe sash tighter around her waist.

She'd hardly slept last night and her nerves were raw.

An hour earlier, she'd awakened, feeling unsettled and more tired than when she went to bed. The cause of her sleeplessness filled her doorway—tanned, clean-shaven, and gorgeous—while she was wearing a ratty old robe she'd had since her school days.

"You'd like to kill me, right?"

"I'm seriously considering it," she said.

"I was in a hurry . . . thinking about something else, I guess. The same thing I thought about all night." He stepped inside and set the pastries on a table. "I was thinking about this." Before she realized what he was doing, he had her in his arms. "Good morning, Elizabeth." Thoroughly, he kissed her on the lips. "That's to make up for the kiss on the forehead."

Her stomach skittered. He was doing it again—so confident, so sure of himself—and she was falling apart inside. With an effort, she willed herself motionless, letting her arms hang limp at her sides. She refused to deal with him and her conflicting emotions at seven o'clock in the morning!

Finally he let go his embrace and stepped back from her. "Where's Ruthie?" he asked.

"She's with Colonel Gordon's family today." Then Elizabeth gave him what she hoped was a friendly smile, but not *too* friendly.

With an affectionate pat on her arm, Jake brushed past her and headed for the kitchen. "Now go finish getting dressed, and I'll meet you in the kitchen."

Fifteen minutes later, she came into the kitchen wearing a beige jersey skirt and a white blouse, an outfit she wore when working outside. She'd caught her hair back and fastened it with a tortoise clasp at the nape of her neck.

He turned from the stove, where he was whisking eggs. "Pretty. I like your hair loose like that."

"What are you doing?" she asked, warmed by the remark.

"Making your breakfast. Any objections?"

Amazed, she watched the man who said all the right things tuck a dish towel around his waist. Minutes later, she had a lighter-than-air omelet on her plate. After the delicious breakfast, while sitting together and sipping coffee, she made out a list of things to take with them to the creek.

"We need to pack sandwiches for lunch and take something along to drink, unless you think we'll be back by then," she said.

"I doubt it. Let's take something just in case."

He had an intensity about him she could almost feel. She'd noticed that when he spoke to the Gypsy men. He seemed to know exactly what he was doing.

Apparently that self-assurance went along with being a Ranger. Carl had respected them because he knew what they trained for. Texas Rangers were the ones who responded first—sometimes the only ones. Many areas had no sheriff, no law enforcement at all except the Rangers. They were the law. Carl used to laugh and say he'd never met a Ranger he liked. If you see Rangers riding up the street, he said, better get inside, because something is about to happen.

"Fort Bliss is a Cavalry post," she said. "What's a Ranger officer doing on staff here?"

"I'm not on staff here," Jake said. "No official connection between Rangers and the Army. We collaborate with each other whenever we need to. I'm ex-Cavalry and served under Colonel Gordon at one time. I loved the Cavalry and went into the Texas Rangers because the state of Texas needed my help. And like the Cavalry, I go where they send me."

Her eyes fixed on him. "So did my husband. Of the seven months we were married, Carl was gone for four of them. The Army is your wife, your mistress, your everything."

"I understand why you feel that way," Jake said, "but I can't agree with you." He drained the last of his coffee and smiled. "The military is a career like any other. At least in the service, a man knows what he does counts for something besides dollars. You're the daughter of a senator. More than most, you know that freedom comes with a price tag. And no matter how high it is, we'll pay it."

She shook her head. "Must be something in the water they give you. Now you sound like my father."

He laughed and pulled her up from the table. "I'm going to need some canoe training today. Are you ready to teach me?"

He didn't try to kiss her again, but instead treated her with a brotherly indifference, as if he'd put her in a little box in the back of his mind. Evidently he could turn his feelings on and off like a spigot. And he definitely didn't want to talk about it.

On their way out the door, her eyes widened. Smiling, she broke into a run for the horse and green wagon parked in front of the house. "Where did you get that canoe? It's beautiful!" she said.

Resting between the side rails was an old birchbark canoe and two paddles. Age had darkened the once-white bark of the canoe to a golden tan color.

"I've never seen one, but have only read about them. That's a real Indian canoe—where did you get it?"

Jake looked pleased by her reaction. "One of the maintenance soldiers got it out of the shed for me. Says it's been here for ten years. Someone, after a raid up north, hauled it back here. It's used a couple of times a year to check the water level of Little Pine Creek. Most places, the creek is only a few feet deep. But where it empties into the Rio Grande, it gets quite deep. As close as the fort is to the Little Pine, flooding can be a problem."

Elizabeth walked around the canoe, admiring the workmanship. "Lovely. It's been well cared for. I'm guessing, but it looks to me like it may be Ojibwa."

"Chippewa," he said. "Same tribe, different pronunciation of their name. How do you know so much about canoes?"

"We belonged to a canoe club in Washington. Lloyd used to race other clubs on the Potomac. Two of my father's friends raced, too. I was little and was so bored. But canoeing is all the rage now." She climbed up onto the wagon seat and set their lunch on the floorboard. "Come on, let's go. I can hardly wait! And remember, Ranger Jake—the fat end of the paddle goes in the water."

∽

The startled cry of a heron and the beat of rushing wings broke the stillness of the marsh. In the stern of the canoe, a mile or so south of Fort Bliss, Elizabeth stroked again with her paddle, synchronizing her movements with Jake's, dipping the paddle in and out of the water in tandem with his. Sunlight poured through the cedars lining the banks of the Little Pine turning the water the color of molten bronze. Not far away, sandy shores littered with logs and upturned roots slipped past, the crumbling ruins of a bygone forest.

An hour earlier, she and Jake had unhitched the horse and left horse and wagon under a tree. Elizabeth carried the lunch and other gear, while Jake lifted the birchbark canoe over his head and walked it to the creek. It didn't weigh more than forty pounds, he told her.

Now Elizabeth dragged her paddle in the water, slowing the canoe. Jake leaned over the bow and grabbed the limb of a dead cedar that had fallen across the stream. Together they worked the canoe beneath the overhanging trunk and coasted by in the shallows. Twice, the canoe scraped bottom.

Jake propelled a clump of floating brush aside with his paddle and grinned at her over his shoulder. "Back home, we'd call this little baby creek a *branch*."

Alongside, the dark green of the pitch pines stood out in contrast to the silvery sandbanks rising above the water. Although they were hundreds of miles from the seashore, creamy white sand lay everywhere, a silent reminder that once upon a time these pine plains rested on the floor of the ocean.

"Glad you came?" she asked.

He nodded. Raising his body slightly, he swung his paddle to the other side and stroked hard. The canoe slipped past a blackened stump submerged in creek water.

"Have to admit," he said, "I wondered back there what you were letting me in for." He dug at the water again.

The black shirt clung to his back, already damp. Behind him, Elizabeth admired the play of muscles in his shoulders and the powerful swell of biceps as he stroked. Watching him paddle, it occurred to her that nearly every Ranger she'd met had been fit and well muscled.

Once again, she found herself wishing he wasn't in the Frontier Battalion.

"Let's check that out." She pointed to the mouth of another creek, which emptied into the Little Pine. They had the whole day to themselves, and she'd decided to let events unfold naturally. They paddled into the inlet, meandering up shallow channels heavy with the smell of wet pine forests. They all led nowhere except to more wild beauty and lonely bogs, a watery wilderness of yellow-scummed swamps and drowning trees.

The silence was profound, broken only by an occasional silver splash of water when a pickerel showed itself. Time and again, they swung the canoe around and paddled back to the Little Pine.

A shaft of sunlight broke through the trees and brushed his hair with fire. In one week, this man had shaken her world to pieces, made her question everything she'd thought and said about men in the last three years. All day she'd waited and watched for him to do or say something stupid, something that would turn her off. He never did.

He was smart and fun to be with—and he liked her, she could tell. She smiled to herself. Knowing that only made her like him more.

They saw few birds and almost no wildlife, except for a lone white-tailed doe at the water's edge. Ears erect and alert, the deer raised its head and looked right at them. Then, slender legs lifting, it turned and bounded up the bank.

Resting her paddle, Elizabeth scanned their surroundings. "No houses, no people, no nothing."

"Which is why some call it the 'pine barren' back here," Jake said. "There are pine barrens and ponds like this from Florida all the way to Texas, running across the southern part of the country."

He was easy to talk to. She found herself telling him things she didn't usually tell people—about her father, about the mother she hardly remembered, about meeting her husband in Washington.

But Jake stiffened every time she mentioned Carl's name.

"The day after you met him, he asked you to marry him, and you said yes? Why?"

Her chin lifted. "I fell in love the minute I saw him."

Shaking his head, Jake replied, "There's no such thing as love at first sight." Then he jerked around and plunged his paddle into the creek again.

She frowned at his back, wondering what happened to his politeness, and what had happened in his life to make him feel this way.

Be careful, she told herself. Up to now, he hadn't so much as mentioned another woman's name.

"Have you ever thought about getting married?" she asked quietly.

Jake tilted his head, but didn't look around to meet her eyes. "Came close, once. Too close. Engaged for over a year. It didn't work out."

That told her exactly nothing. "Was she beautiful?"

She caught the tensing of his shoulders and realized she'd touched a nerve. Obviously he wasn't interested in discussing the subject.

"Sorry, Jake, I shouldn't have brought it up. It's none of my business."

He snapped his head around, his paddle dragging the water. "She broke it off, not me, although I would have with the next breath. Her name is Audrey and, yes, she's beautiful. Or was. Tall, with pitch-black hair, and a few years older than me. She was as sophisticated as they come."

The lines in his face hardened. "I was eighteen when I met her, a young green lieutenant with a new command and feeling ten feet tall. The kid from Burkburnett fell for her hard and then bought her a ring. . . ."

His voice trailed off. She said nothing, sensing he hadn't finished.

A few moments later, he said, "I wanted a big church

wedding, with her folks, my folks, all my aunts, uncles, and cousins trekking up to Houston to see us get married. My favorite uncle is a Methodist minister. He was coming out from Mobile to perform the ceremony."

His mouth tightened and the muscles of his jaw worked. When he turned back to face her, his expression was aloof. "I thought we were happy. I loved her, or thought I did, and I never suspected anything wrong until the day I walked in on her with another man."

Elizabeth felt as if a bucket of ice water had been dumped on her head. "I'm sorry, Jake."

"So was I. In the year or so that I knew her, I never looked at another woman. My mother's marriage wasn't good, and I was determined to make mine different. I wanted to be married to one woman for the rest of my life. Till death us do part and all that. Instead, I didn't even make it to the altar."

"You must've been so hurt."

"I got over it." His voice was flat.

"When you didn't talk about it, I guessed something like that had happened."

One corner of his mouth dug in. "Only you figured it was the other way around, that it was me with other women."

Elizabeth looked away. "I'm sorry about that, too." Murky water rippled around the stern of the canoe. Elizabeth looked at it, uneasy about what was coming.

His paddle strokes increased—deeper, stronger, knifing the dark water as if in a hurry to leave this spot as soon as he could.

Another hard plunge forced the canoe ahead.

He held the paddle up at the top of his swing, poised for another plunge into the water. Then slowly, deliberately, he slipped the paddle into the water without a ripple and resumed his lazy yet powerful strokes.

They paddled on in silence. After a moment he turned and smiled over his shoulder at her. He dipped his fingers in the creek and flicked water back at her.

"There's something I didn't tell you," he said. "I'm no stranger to falling in love at first sight. I've been burned. You beat me by an hour or two, but I was way ahead of Carl. I was down on my knees and proposing to Audrey just three hours after I met her."

Though he smiled when he said it, there was something in his voice that said he wasn't about to make that mistake again.

Paddling on, they talked easily about everything—except Carl.

A white heron stood motionless in the water, stalking minnows in the shallows by the bank. The skinny, long-legged little bird peered down, then lifted each little stick leg in slow motion, setting a tiny foot down with such delicacy it never muddied the water.

Elizabeth felt an odd kinship with the bird, because she was trying to choose her words as carefully as the heron was choosing its footsteps.

And Carl muddied the water.

Elizabeth pointed her paddle forward. "I'm getting tired of sitting. How about we paddle around that next bend and then pull in, stretch our legs a little?"

They beached the canoe and, hand in hand, began to walk the wide sandy trail that served as a road through the thick growth of trees.

Hugging her shoulder, he looked up at the trees and blew

out a sigh. "Thanks for bringing me here, Elizabeth. I hadn't realized how tense I was. I needed this."

∞

A little more than an hour later, they beached the canoe again, this time to have lunch. Sitting together in the shade of a huge tree, they devoured the sandwiches and drank every drop of the lemonade they'd brought along.

Afterward, Jake lay back on the grass, hands folded under his head. The sun felt warm on his face. Pitch gum cooking in the nearby pines drenched the air with the tang of turpentine. With a contented grunt, he closed his eyes.

The grass rustled alongside as Elizabeth dropped down beside him. He opened his eyes and stared through the branches at a patch of blue sky overhead.

"Suzanne told me you'd been wounded," she said. "When did that happen?"

"Long time ago. An Apache hit me with a bullet to my hip."

"Where were you?"

Jake shifted to his side and looked at her. "Kansas," he answered. "I was part of a rescue operation with the Fourth Cavalry. I'd gone back onto the field after a wounded man when I was shot."

"But there must be more to it than that," she said.

Reluctantly, Jake went on to tell her the whole story. He'd been a lieutenant then and had gone searching for his missing commander, now Colonel Gordon. The Cavalry had come in fast over a hill north of Fort Dodge after the Apaches, who scattered under the onslaught of three companies of soldiers. It was a shootout, both sides taking fire.

Jake rode off across the field, really a valley between two

mountains, when he spotted the colonel. He yelled to him to grab his arm. Jake slowed the horse and made two passes before he hooked the colonel's arm and got a good hold on him.

It was on the second pass he was shot. Bloody from the waist down and so woozy he couldn't see straight, he rode back to his unit, half dragging, half carrying his commander.

After hearing the story, Elizabeth studied him for a moment, her eyes dark with questions. "When you went in, were the Indians shooting at you?"

"Of course they were."

"And you still went in?"

"I was the team's leader, and my job was to get a wounded man out. We try never to leave a man behind. Wounded or dead, he goes out with us." He spoke the words in a flat, calm voice.

The color drained from her face. She moved closer to him, reached over and took his hand in hers.

"You're crazy, you know that," she said.

He smiled and squeezed her hand. *Crazy about you.*

Inside, he was kicking himself. He hadn't told her of Colonel Gordon's offer to come back to the Cavalry and work with him and his battalions. It was a good opportunity for him, putting him on the fast track for promotion. He didn't know how she'd react to that. Maybe they both needed more time.

He rolled his head to the side and gazed at the dark windblown hair and the beautiful features he couldn't get out of his mind.

Don't push your luck.

Maybe he'd tell her on the way home. . . .

And yet telling her was the last thing he wanted to do.

He sat up. "Let's get back on the water," he said.

Eighteen

THEY WERE ON THE WATER less than ten minutes when she saw it: a two-foot-high mass of limbs and stones plastered with mud, stretching across the creek from bank to bank. Water pooled behind it, deepening.

Elizabeth squealed. "A beaver dam—that's it. This is what Gus saw. We found it."

"They'll have to send a detail out here and tear it down," Jake said. "This is all Fort Bliss property. They can't leave it to flood."

Elizabeth held back, studying the sluggish water this side of the dam and the foam-flecked baby rapids tumbling through a yard-wide channel, an opening where the current had cut through.

She pursed her lips thoughtfully. "If we're ever going to swamp, it'll be now."

Jake's paddle stopped midair. He turned. "How do we get around it?"

She pointed to the opening. "We don't. We let the current take us through. Should be okay. Just steer for that channel in the middle." She giggled. "And stop frowning. The water's barely three feet deep. It's just a little beaver dam."

Jake began paddling hard for the sluice of water. Too hard. And things went very wrong, very fast. They overshot the current in the center of the creek, crossed it, and wound up in the still eddies behind the dam.

"Back in the current—back in the current!" Elizabeth swept the water behind her, paddling backward frantically.

Lifting himself for leverage, Jake strained and fought the water forward.

"Other way!" she hollered.

Elizabeth's eyes widened on something behind him. He spun around.

The dam rushed at them.

Faced with an imminent collision, he did what any good soldier would do. He rammed it with his weapon. The paddle snapped, the blade flipping end over end and plopping in the water. With a scraping sound, the bow of the canoe plowed into the mud and sticks of the dam.

Dumbfounded, Jake looked at Elizabeth, gripping his broken piece of paddle like a broom handle.

She doubled over with laughter.

"This is not funny, Elizabeth!"

The current sucked the stern of the canoe back out into the channel. Elizabeth fell to her knees, backstroking with her paddle. The creek poured in over the side. "We're swamping!"

Jake launched himself over the side. In a small avalanche of stones and twigs, he scrambled onto the beaver dam and stretched for the canoe. The ground sagged beneath him. His legs caved through and plunged him knee-deep in mud. He swiped for the canoe as he went down, grabbing the bow with both hands. Straining, feet rooted in the dry inner chamber of the beaver lodge, he tried to wrest the twelve-foot canoe awash with brown water from the clutches of the Little Pine.

All around them, furry beaver heads surfaced like corks and began swimming toward shore. Whapping her tail, an irate mother beaver scampered around Jake and the hole he'd made in her kitchen ceiling.

With a groan, the canoe wrenched from his hands and drifted out into the current. Elizabeth floated away. The current sucked the stern around into the strip of white water gurgling through the dam. Elizabeth rode the canoe backward into the pool at the foot of the dam, where the canoe promptly filled up and sank. Sitting in the creek, the water up to her neck, she squirted a stream of water through her teeth and grabbed for her hat as it floated by. She missed.

Jake heaved the useless piece of paddle into the woods on the other side of the creek and waded through the water after her. He hauled her to her feet. "You all right?"

Muddy water dripped from the end of her nose. Picking a handful of hair away from her mouth, she laughed. "Good thing you didn't join the Navy."

"True," he said. "Well, there goes your hat."

Holding his elbows out of the water, Jake slogged after the hat and the rest of their things that had floated away. Together they got the canoe up to the surface. Effortlessly Jake raised the canoe and flipped it, dumping out all the water. Setting the canoe back on the water, he dragged himself over the side, then helped her in.

Immediately they started to argue over who was going to sit where.

"Sit in the bow, Jake!"

"No, I'm going to paddle."

"Sorry, you broke yours. The person in the stern steers and you don't know how. So you ride up front back to the Fort."

"I will not be just a passenger," he said, then grabbed the paddle from her hands, crawled back to the stern, and plunked himself down onto the middle seat. "You are not paddling me back to the fort." He stripped off his wet shirt and turned to spread it to dry on the small deck behind him.

She shook her head. "Don't be ridiculous, Jake. Give me that paddle."

"Let's look at this logically—I'm bigger and have more strength."

Her voice scaled up. "No. I want to paddle."

"Elizabeth, please . . ."

Muttering under her breath, she began moving up to the bow. The canoe rocked wildly.

Eyes wide, Jake gripped both sides of the canoe. "Good. Now sit down before you swamp us again."

Turning on him, she said, "Stop treating me like a private!"

"Stop fussing at me and sit still."

She glared at him. "Is that another order?"

"No, ma'am." He grinned at her. "Consider it a firm request. C'mon, I need your help."

Finally she took her seat. "You always have to be in charge, don't you?"

"Most of the time, that's what I get paid for. But not

with you. If I was in charge now, we'd be somewhere on land, nice and dry."

Pretending to ignore him, she settled herself in the bow, with her back to him.

She almost missed it. A small furry head, bobbing alongside the canoe. Tiny front legs pedaling the water, it struggled to stay afloat. Twice the little head went under.

"Jake, wait! Let's get this little guy out of the water. He's going to drown." She leaned out over the side of the canoe.

"All right, but be careful or we'll tip over again."

"He doesn't swim very well. May be only a day or two old." She stretched her hand down into the water.

Jake grabbed the back of her dress to keep her in the canoe.

"There, I got him!" She scooped the small beaver out of the water and put it in her lap. He lay still, his eyes half closed. "Oh, the poor little thing. Take us back to the dam and let's put him with the others. We have to find its mother." She twisted around and looked up at Jake.

Jake stared at her. "Are you serious? You want me to turn around and paddle back to the beaver dam I fell through and put this animal back?"

"Please," she said softly.

Shaking his head, he turned the canoe and headed back to the broken dam. The beavers had returned and were swimming around their collapsed lodge.

Jake swung his legs over the side and dropped into the water alongside the dam. "You are aware, of course, that beavers have big teeth?"

"Which is why you have to keep your distance. Return the baby and we'll leave."

"Give him to me," he said, and held out his hand.

Elizabeth eased the little animal up and gingerly laid the little ball of wet fur in Jake's palm.

"Not very big, is he?" Jake said.

For all his gruffness, he held the baby beaver gently as he scrambled toward the dam. He stumbled twice and slid sideways, but the hand holding the tiny beaver stayed steady.

The little thing squeaked. Immediately a larger beaver raised its head and looked in their direction. She moved toward Jake, slow and wary. Jake set the baby down on a dry section of the dam and then carefully backed away.

∞

A half hour later, Elizabeth turned and asked Jake, "Was that thunder?"

He cocked his head. In the stillness, a blue jay called, one shrill, piercing note before it flew off into the woods. To the east, a mountain of dark Pacific thunderheads boiled overhead. A low, rolling rumble thumped across the sky.

"There's your answer," he said.

Wind gusted a line of small whitecaps up the Little Pine. Soon the waves began slapping up against their canoe. Raindrops pelted rings across the water. Jake reached behind him, grabbed her hat and his shirt. Juggling the paddle, he yanked the shirt on over his head, then started paddling for shore.

He glanced at the sky. "Put your shoes on, and let's get out of this canoe. I don't like the looks of this."

Jake paddled intently, his eyes scanning the bank alongside. A jagged tree of lightning blazed above the creek. The Little Pine's surface glowed with luminescence, as though lit from below. All along the creek banks, the cedar tips pulsed an eerie blue. A peculiar odor hung in the air.

Ozone.

Jake dropped to one knee and dug hard for the nearest bank. With one last, mighty shove of the paddle, he stood, drawing Elizabeth up with him. The canoe surged for the shore.

The sky exploded into blinding brilliance.

"Jump!"

∽

Jake landed in the water a few feet behind Elizabeth and shoved her up the bank ahead of him. He hauled the canoe up onto the bank and turned it upside down in the weeds.

They broke into a run, heading for cover. He stumbled, grabbed a tree trunk for balance, and started running again.

She shot him a concerned look. "You're limping. What's wrong?"

"I twisted my ankle when I fell through the beaver dam. Keep going! Let's get out of these trees!"

Squinting into the wind, he zigzagged them through the woods, away from the canoe, away from the creek. A quarter mile later, they found one of the sand roads that cut through the pines.

Overhead, lightning lit the sky, and rain came down in torrents. Every few seconds, thunder crashed. On both sides of the road, the trees thrashed under the force of the wind.

Elizabeth screamed when a bolt of lightning flashed from a mile high. With a great cracking sound, the trunk of a nearby cedar split its length and fell across the road, blackened, smoking in the rain.

"We're right in the middle of it!" Jake shouted. "Look for someplace open . . . Over there!" He grabbed her hand and led her toward a small meadow of stumps and dunes on the other side of the road.

A washed-out gully lay between them and safety. It wasn't wide, but he wouldn't risk jumping it with a bad ankle. If something happened to him, she'd be completely on her own. He squatted, then slid on his behind down into the gully.

Elizabeth leaped across the gully and spun around. "How are you going to get out of there?"

"I'll find a way. Keep running—don't wait for me." He stretched for a broken stump near the top, but couldn't quite reach it. He kicked his good foot into the side of the bank for a toehold.

Lightning flashed again, painting her face a glassy silver. Worried for her, he yelled at her to run. "Elizabeth," he shouted. "Go!"

But thunder drowned out his words.

To his surprise, she leaped down into the ditch with him.

He reached for the stump again, but missed. He looked up in disbelief. Six months before, he and his team had scaled a mountain of near vertical rock. They'd hauled over the top, guns blazing, and captured a gang of train robbers.

And now he couldn't get himself out of a ditch!

Splashing behind him, Elizabeth stooped and shoved a shoulder under his hip, lifting. "Grab it now!"

He strained for the stump at the top of the ditch. This time he managed to wrap first one, then both hands around its rough bark. He hung there, half in, half out of the ditch.

Elizabeth scrambled up his back, climbing him like a ladder, using his hips and shoulders as steps. At the top she turned and grabbed both of his elbows and pulled. Twice her feet skidded out from under her and she fell hard on her behind.

"You're going to hurt yourself. You're not strong enough!"

That got him an angry look.

∞

Elizabeth dragged him a few inches more. It was enough. He got his good leg under him, crawled over the top, and staggered to his feet. He took her hand and rushed toward the clearing, lightning stabbing all around them. In the center, Jake dove to the ground with her behind a sand dune.

Chest heaving, Elizabeth clutched him and blinked up into the rain, watching the war in the sky. Thunder boomed.

He grinned. "Scared?"

She made a face at him. "If it weren't for me, you'd still be in the ditch. And no, I'm not scared. *Terrified* is more like it." Her heart raced, thumping as if it might jump right out of her rib cage.

He tucked her head under his chin and banded his arms tightly around her.

"I've never seen a storm as wild as this," she said.

"It's been hot here all week, and the heat triggers them off." He studied the sky. "It won't last long."

His pants and shirt were drenched, plastered to his body. Yet, wet as he was, she felt the body heat radiating from him. The man was a furnace. Arms wrapped around him, she pressed closer against the unyielding hardness of his chest.

The deep-down shakiness she felt reminded her how close they'd come to getting killed. The adrenaline was still flooding her veins. His too.

Another flash of lightning made her hide her face in his neck. Her nose pushed against solid flesh. Even his neck was hard. There was no softness to this man. Under the wet black shirt, he was a brick wall. His arms tightened protectively around her. Over his shoulder she peeked at the sky. Despite the thunder, the pouring rain, and being frightened half to death, she had to admit the firm grip of masculine hands holding her was reassuring.

Jake plucked a wet strand of hair from her cheek and smoothed it behind her ear. "Are you all right?"

Her breath sucked in at the husky catch in his voice. The man in her arms was big and strong and quiet.

"You're just about the bravest man I've ever met."

His head fell back and he burst out laughing. "And you're beautiful when you're wet—and scared to death," he said, gray eyes creased half shut by his smile.

She melted inside. None of this made sense. She was curled up with a Texas Ranger, but at that moment, what he did for a living seemed unimportant.

They held each other, reluctant to break the spell of the moment.

⌒

Finally he drew a deep breath, pulled back, and traced a wet streak down her cheek, "Is this rain or tears?"

"Both, I guess. I was so scared."

"We both were."

"I thought maybe it was just me."

He stroked the back of her head, awed by how she made him feel.

When she moved closer against him, he smiled. She seemed almost as happy as he was.

And yet there had been times when Audrey had seemed happy with him, too.

This was not the time to think about *her*. He hoped Elizabeth wasn't thinking about Carl.

Everything inside him went still. He didn't move, didn't speak. If Elizabeth was still in love with Evans, what was building between them meant nothing.

"When I was holding you"—he almost had to force the words out—"were you thinking of me or of Carl?"

Elizabeth sat up and pushed her hair back from her face, her eyes troubled. "You can't believe I was thinking of him then."

"It crossed my mind."

"Why?"

He propped himself on an elbow and looked down at her. The words, raw and ragged, tore out of him before he could stop them. "I know you loved him."

Elizabeth sighed as she caressed the side of his face. "Of course I loved him. I married him. But I never thought of him today. Not once. I was thinking about you and how you made me feel."

He looked up as faraway thunder rumbled. The storm was passing, leaving in its wake a gentle rain. In the distance, bright sunlight spoked through the clouds.

Elizabeth said softly, "Carl is gone. I've accepted that." Then she turned his face to hers and kissed him.

"Then why do you still wear his ring?"

She smiled. "When was the last time you looked?"

He pulled her hand from his cheek and turned it over,

then ran his thumb across the band of white skin where her wedding ring had been. "When did you take it off?"

"Last night—after you brought me home."

He pulled her into his arms and held her close. "Something's going on between us," he said. "Forget what I said about Carl. I had no right to say it. It won't happen again. I'll deal with it. Maybe it's this storm. I don't know what's wrong with me."

Looking down at his arm, he brushed gritty streaks of sand away. He was jealous of her dead husband, that's what was wrong with him. Worse, he was in over his head with her—the last thing he'd meant to do. And that raised all sorts of complications with the Rangers, with her father, with himself. With her.

He saw some unsettling similarities with how he felt about Elizabeth and how he'd felt about Audrey when he first met her. The instant attraction, for one. Anger coursed through him at the thought. Elizabeth was *nothing* like her. Elizabeth was honest.

He didn't know how he was going to do this or how it would all turn out.

For the first time in his life, he didn't want to know.

∞

The ride back to Fort Bliss to return the canoe was quiet, both of them lost in their own thoughts. When Jake reached across and covered her hand with his, Elizabeth realized that neither of them had spoken a word for a long while.

"Tired?" he asked.

"A little."

It was a mystery to her how he'd done it. For three years

she'd managed to avoid men like him. That hadn't been easy. Then this slow-talking Texas Ranger broke through the barriers she'd built around her heart. Apparently, Jake Nelson didn't understand that the nature of walls was to keep people like him out. He blew right through them, over them, around them.

Forget finesse. Texas Rangers bulled their way in.

And military? Though he wasn't in the Army now, he had been and he'd loved it. He'd left it only because he loved Texas more, and the Rangers needed him. This afternoon, as if putting her on notice, he'd told her he was already approved for the rank of major, to work as Colonel Gordon's XO, which put him second-in-command of the battalion.

She suspected his upcoming promotion was only the next step for him. At this rate, he'd make full colonel before he was forty.

She glanced at the strong profile of her driver and suppressed a sigh. For Carl, the military had been a job. But it ran deeper than that for Jake, much deeper. For him, it was almost a calling. He was committed to serving his country. The Army was one way. Texas Rangers and the law was another. Thank heavens there were men like him, but she had no intention of marrying one.

"You ever think about leaving the Rangers early?" she asked, keeping her voice casual.

"Leaving? Yes. Early, no. I'll finish what I signed on for."

"And then what?"

"If I pass up the Army's offer, I'm thinking about going into law enforcement."

She turned and looked out at the passing landscape.

Jake pulled her hand across and wound his fingers through

hers. He heaved a sigh. "You're trying to figure us out. So am I. But I don't know where to start. As a former officer's wife, you've got all the answers to anything I say to try to change your mind about me and what I do."

The words pulled from him reluctantly, as if he hadn't planned to say them. He was quiet for a minute, then brought her hand to his lips and kissed it.

"I like being with you, talking with you, even fussing with you, and it's only fair you know something else: I'm not going to let you run away because of what I do for a living. Not without a fight."

Though he smiled when he said it, the broad jaw was squared off.

Love me at your own risk, it seemed to say.

Careful, she told herself. Men like Jake played to win.

Nineteen

CAMPO MILITAR NO. 13
CHIHUAHUA, MEXICO

THE WIND WAS PICKING UP, and it had started to rain again.
From the window of his walnut-paneled office at the front
of the building, General Manuel Diego watched the activity
at the gate below.

Every few minutes, mule teams pulled another yellow-
brown Mexican Army wagon through the gates. Guards
waved them toward the open area for the stables behind
the buildings. The soldier drivers of the big wagons leaned
forward, shouting and cracking whips, hurrying to get out
of the weather.

Diego leaned forward and peered down. His mouth tightened. A security guard in a black raincoat was questioning
the rider on a gray horse stopped at the gate.

The rider was Major Ramon Chavez, who had precipi-
tated the crisis in El Paso when he seized an unknown
American woman hostage at the courthouse to get himself

out alive. The woman, unfortunately, turned out to be the sister of the slain editor and the daughter of a prominent U.S. senator.

What rotten luck!

Diego knew exactly what Chavez had come to talk about.

An unexpected tip had come to Diego that morning, saying that the American woman and her three Ranger rescuers had made it safely out of Mexico. Diego sat down at his desk and waited for his visitor to enter his office.

He glanced at the humidor on his desk, filled with pungent black cigars, snug in their paper jackets. He picked one up, rolled it between his fingers, then sighed and put it back. He was fifty-seven now, and his wife was on him all the time about the smoking.

Despite his years, he looked strong and muscular and still possessed the beefsteak shoulders of a once-powerful physique. Thick iron gray hair swept back from a deeply tanned face.

He was a walking encyclopedia of Mexican military structure and disagreed with President Hector Guevara on almost everything the overeducated bleeding heart, as he called him, tried to do. A firm hand—General Manuel Diego's hand—was what was needed with Indians and peasants both. Toughness. An occasional slap down by the Army always helped. He was almost ready. For two years he'd been working the countryside, and he already had much support. A distraction, a dustup with the United States, would muddy the picture enough that Diego's troops could take over the capital before Guevara knew what was happening.

This unplanned abduction of the editor's sister by the

irritating man coming up the stairs to his office threatened everything.

He reached into a candy dish alongside the humidor and took out a piece of toffee. He sucked on the sweetness instead of smoking. His wife had a nose like a bloodhound.

There was a light knock at the door. Major Ramon Chavez, brushing himself off, strode into the room, his scarred face wet with rain.

"What happened the other day?" the general growled. "How did they slip by you?"

Mopping his face with a handkerchief, Major Chavez paced over to the window and back. "Same as always. The Rangers have connections in this country. They show up in Mexico, do what they came to do, then disappear. It's like they never existed."

Diego frowned. "From what I hear, these Rangers are pushy and bold, act almost like police."

"They're Texas Rangers. In Texas, they *are* police, every one of them," Chavez said. His face took on a strained look, the scar tight, like a stretched rubber band. "Someone in the U.S. sent this telegram to President Guevara," he said, and handed it to Diego.

Face flushing, Diego read the telegram, then tossed it on the desk. A gust of wind swept across the grounds outside. With a sound like thrown rice, rain pelted the windows of his office. After a moment, he looked up at a waiting Major Chavez.

Chavez nodded. "There's more. President Guevara's answer to that telegram was, 'Good. I'll knot the rope myself.'"

Diego swore. "And when I throw him out of office, I'll return the favor." He scooped up the telegram, read it again, then looked at the major. "They have positive Ranger identifications of me and you in San Jose when we brought the bodies back. Says when and if we enter Texas again, they'll charge us with the murder of the editor Lloyd Madison."

Just beneath the surface, mute anger was building. Diego grabbed a cigar from the humidor and bit the end off. Wetting the cigar between his lips, he struck a match, held it steady, and puffed until the tip glowed.

Chavez picked up the copy of the *Grande Examiner* on Diego's desk. "This was her brother's paper. It's hers now. I heard she's doing a special edition on us and the coming revolt in Mexico. And you."

"I don't think she'll be around that long." Diego leaned back in his chair. Lips pursed, he puffed and sent three perfect smoke rings circling for the ceiling. "If what I'm planning works, I think we can eliminate Elizabeth Evans with not a hint of military involvement."

Twenty

THE FOLLOWING WEEK
FORT BLISS EMERGENCY ROOM

"HELLO. WHAT TIME TONIGHT, and what are you wearing?"
Elizabeth asked as she came through the door. She'd stopped
by the hospital before she left for El Paso. She needed to
check when they planned to leave for the band concert to
be sure she got back in time.

The Fourth Cavalry military band was giving a concert
in Riverside Park in El Paso, a weekly event the whole
town looked forward to. Free entertainment, compliments
of Fort Bliss.

The relationship between El Paso and Fort Bliss was a
special one. For years, the nearby Army post had protected
the territory from marauding Indians. El Paso reciprocated
by donating money, land, and sites for a new fort every time
the government wanted to move it—including one site right
downtown. El Paso wanted her fort as close as she could
get it. When the railroads came in and laid the tracks right

up the middle of the fort's parade grounds, the city council shook their heads. A minor inconvenience. A nearby fort with a large payroll and lots of guns meant safety and a thriving economy for the town.

They were on Site Number Five, and El Paso had its fingers crossed that the government didn't move it again.

At her desk, Suzanne put her pencil down and looked up from a patient's chart. "The escort wagon leaves at six from the commissary. And I'm wearing nothing fancy, just a skirt and blouse."

She leaned forward on her elbows and rubbed her eyes. "My feet hurt," she said. "I spent the whole crazy morning running back and forth to doctors in different examining rooms, taping up sprained or broken ankles. One man had a sprained toe. How does one go about spraining a toe?"

Basic Training was winding down and the Infantry companies were into the mandatory fifteen-mile road marches. As a result, half of Fort Bliss was hobbling.

Suzanne folded her arms and smiled at Elizabeth. "What do you hear from the infamous B-Team?"

"See some of them every day, usually Jake, unless he's tied up, like today. You have anyone specific in mind—like Gus Dukker?" She gave Suzanne a wide-eyed, innocent look.

"Of course not," Suzanne answered quickly.

Elizabeth raised an eyebrow. Master Sergeant Gus Dukker had been appearing every day in the Emergency Room to pass along some trivial message from Jake to Elizabeth. And to hang around Suzanne.

Elizabeth smiled and motioned her head toward the front door. "Mention his name and look who waltzes through the door."

"I didn't mention his name," Suzanne muttered.

With a loose-boned, rolling walk, Gus ambled across the waiting room, pulling off his gloves.

Suzanne rolled her eyes. "He drives me nuts."

"He's cute, though."

Suzanne sniffed. "You think a streetcar's cute. If he'd just be serious once in a while, instead of teasing all the time."

"Then pay some attention to him," Elizabeth said quietly. "That's what he wants."

"Morning, ladies," Gus said as he approached the desk.

"I'm being stood up for lunch again, right?" Elizabeth said.

Gus nodded and checked his watch. "Boss is probably in El Paso with the police chief as we speak. Seems he wants to keep the bad Mexican kids in Juarez where they belong, not El Paso."

Elizabeth shrugged. "I figured something like that as soon as you walked in."

"Jake said he'll be back in plenty of time for the concert tonight. We don't have to leave the post until six. It'll take close to an hour to get to town. He said to tell you the escort driver will pick up everyone at the commissary."

Gus turned to Suzanne and grinned. "How you doing, Suzanne? I'm going to drive Elizabeth into town and back, but I'm free for lunch . . . if you were to ask me, that is."

"Sorry, I'm on a diet," she said.

"I can see why."

Her back stiff, she turned and started for the door.

Gus held his hand out. "Just teasing."

"You'll notice I'm not laughing," she said, and walked away.

∞

That evening, as always, the Fourth Cavalry Regimental Band was a crowd-pleaser. People came from miles around to listen to a special March Program that had everyone tapping their feet to the stirring music. Everyone loved the marches and were on their feet clapping and cheering for several minutes afterward. The conductor and the band stood and took three bows.

More entertainment followed when the Fourth Cavalry's bugler stepped onstage in his fancy dress uniform and played a familiar bugle call on his shiny bugle.

"El Paso, which one was that?" the bugler called.

"Charge!" the crowd shouted back.

Then came a couple more familiar calls: "Reveille!" and "Taps!"

But the next ones he played were all met with puzzled looks and absolute silence. The bugler laughed. "Never heard those before, have you?" He made a loud, rude *blat* on his horn. "Those calls were instructions to the horses: Right, Walk Forward, Trot, Gallop, Turn Around, Halt, and Lie Down. In a battle, with all the noise and gunfire, they can't hear shouted orders. Cavalry horses know these calls and many more! Come out to the post and watch our horses drill. And while you're out there, if you hear the bugler sound 'Feeding Time at the Stable,' get out of the way!"

The audience howled and clapped.

As the Rangers were leaving, the escort driver who had brought them in pushed through the crowd to his group of men and women, military and civilians, waiting for their ride back to Fort Bliss.

"This place was so crowded tonight, I had to use a livery six blocks away," he said. "Be at least thirty minutes before I get the teams hitched and get back here."

Ranger Jose Martinez, half Navajo and half Mexican, was Company B's communication specialist. A short man with a crooked grin, he spoke seven languages, including most of the major Indian ones. He turned and said to the others, "Got an idea. Let's duck this crowd and walk with him to the livery. My backside's asleep anyway."

Elizabeth wheeled around, smiling. Walking to the livery was a great idea. She was having a good time and in no hurry to get back to the post. This was the first time they'd all gone out together. She'd looked forward to this night, to getting Jake away from the Annex and his responsibilities, to just being a normal man for a few hours. The band concert in El Paso that night had been the perfect excuse.

Jake and the teams worked most days. Sometimes they had special assignments, but lately their work in El Paso concentrated on apprehending outlaws and Mexican bandits. Although he oversaw all the groups, he worked with B Company, his old company when he could. Occasionally they trained from dawn to dusk and right through dinner.

Twice, Elizabeth took pity on them and cooked at Jake's place for the ten of them. After eating, they fell asleep on the couch or on the floor.

She looked over at Gus, still studying the line of carriages in the street. Twice he never left the table after dinner, but instead pushed his plate aside, folded his arms on the table, and laid his head down, asleep in seconds.

The only times he'd stayed awake were the nights Suzanne ate with them.

Elizabeth turned to Suzanne, standing alongside her. "Want to walk to the livery with them?"

Gus took Suzanne's arm. "Sure, she does. She needs the exercise."

Suzanne jerked her arm away, dark hair flying. "Why don't you come right out and say it—you think I'm fat!"

"Aw, I do not. I never said that." A slow, teasing grin crinkled his eyes.

They were at it again, Elizabeth thought as she narrowed her eyes at Gus.

∞

She and Suzanne both wore white skirts that night, Elizabeth with an orange shirt and a matching silk scarf holding her hair back. Suzanne wore dangly earrings and a ribbed pink top out over her skirt. She'd knotted the sleeves of a pink sweater around her waist, partly to hide her hips, Elizabeth thought with a pang.

Suzanne wasn't fat; she just thought she was. And Gus wasn't helping.

Jose Martinez and their driver dodged across the street. The rest of the team, Elizabeth, and Suzanne followed, threading between the stopped buggies.

Jake's hand closed around Elizabeth's arm as they stepped off the sidewalk and didn't let go until they were across the street. Gus did the same with Suzanne, who shook him off as soon as they reached the other side.

Their driver turned off busy Second Street onto Tunnel Street at the next intersection, leaving the bright lights of the pavilion and Riverside Park behind. The sidewalk ahead of them was empty, people heading down other streets for the other liveries.

Five years ago, in 1881, when four major railroads laid tracks into El Paso, the little border town mushroomed overnight. The seedier parts of town, like this section of Tunnel Street, hadn't been upgraded yet. The business section of El Paso now had paved sidewalks with curbs, sewers, electric lights in most stores, and even a few telephones. But not Tunnel Street.

The farther they went down Tunnel, the more dilapidated the neighborhood became. The wooden sidewalks were littered and broken in places. Some storefronts had roll-down metal shades and iron gates in the doorways. Two closed businesses had boards nailed over the windows.

A tall older boy in baggy trousers and a floppy shirt leaned against a lamppost and smirked at the girls as they passed. A green bandanna trailed from a pocket. As they passed, he pulled it out and dusted his hands with it.

Gus made a growl in his throat.

Suzanne glanced up. "What's wrong?"

"Nothing. The rest of you catch that scarf thing?" he said quietly.

"Yeah," Jake said. "Stay alert. Could be a signal."

Halfway down the block, another young man lounged against a building. This one was slightly older, twenty or so. He stood there smoking, watching them. He also wore baggy pants and had a green bandanna, knotted at the back of his neck. He patted his head as they passed.

Chalked words and odd symbols were everywhere, scribbled on walls and doors, even on sidewalks. As Elizabeth studied the chalk pictures, a press release from the newspaper syndicate on the telegraph ran across her mind. It had been an article on the growing number of big-city street gangs in Baltimore, San Francisco, and New Orleans, and how to recognize them.

She squeezed Jake's arm. "I'm no expert, but some of that writing looks like gang markers to me."

Jake turned his head slowly from side to side. "This whole setup is strange. It doesn't fit. Most gangs are obvious in how they advertise themselves. But this I don't understand. Looks like a child's scribbling."

Three doors down, on the other side of the street, someone shifted deeper into a darkened doorway, a flow of black in black. Jose shot his hand out and snapped a downward gesture. Jake repeated the signal for the men behind.

"Jose doesn't like it, either," he said.

"Neither do I," said Gus.

Fred looked over from the other side. "We all picked it up."

Down the street, five dark figures slipped out of doorways, speaking Spanish. Chains wrapped their fists.

"Uh-oh," Jake said. He led Elizabeth across in front of him and tucked her close against his left side.

Wide-eyed, Elizabeth looked at him. "Why did you do that?"

"Freeing my right hand in case I need it."

Elizabeth glanced over her shoulder. "Gus didn't move Suzanne."

"Because he's left-handed."

Behind her, she heard Gus quietly telling Suzanne the same. Suzanne looked surprised when he put his arm around her and pulled her close against his right side.

"Suzanne . . ." he started.

"Now what?"

His mouth tightened. "Nothing. Just stay close to me."

He closed the distance between the two of them and Jake and Elizabeth ahead. Though nothing had been said, Fred Barkley and Bronco Butler, originally from Montana, moved forward, staggering themselves, one on Elizabeth's exposed left, the other on Suzanne's right. Each woman was now flanked by two Rangers.

Jose Martinez shoved their driver behind him and stepped out in front of the Ranger group.

"*Hola, amigos. Qué pasa?*" Jose called to the group of toughs.

A long burst of Spanish came back, accompanied by fist shaking by the older boys blocking the sidewalk. All wore the uniform of baggy pants and floppy shirts with green bandannas. Their leader, a man in his mid-twenties, had a chain tattooed around his neck. He pointed at Elizabeth and shouted.

Never taking his eyes off Chain Man, Jose said to the others, "They say they're *Arroyos*. If they are, that's bad news. Arroyos are junior partners of a big Indian street gang in Mexico City."

"When they get older, they move up with the big boys," Gus said. "Guns and street crime. Despite who they say they are, most of these so-called kids are grown men in pretty good condition. They don't fit the picture."

"Watch how they move," Jake said. "They're erect and straight-backed. It almost looks as if they're military."

"What do they want from us?" Gus asked Jose.

"I don't know yet. I understand their dialect. They've

pointed back and forth to the girls, but don't know their names. They're confused about who's who."

"Think they're after Elizabeth again?" Jake asked, his voice cold.

Jose studied the gang in front of them and shrugged. "Makes as much sense as anything else. Two of the boys have Kali sticks—Filipino fighting sticks—behind them. They may be young, but they're mean. They say we're part of the Victors, a rival gang in Juarez. Seems that orange scarf on Elizabeth's head is the Victors' color. I don't believe that. They're not very convincing. I think it's just an excuse to attack us."

Elizabeth snatched the scarf from her head, stuffed it into her skirt pocket.

"Let's try to talk our way out first," Jake said to Jose. "Tell them we're soldiers on our way back to Fort Bliss, that we don't want trouble from them or anyone else. Tell them also we can hurt them."

Jose translated, using their Mexican dialect. One shirtless youngster of fourteen or so wore a green necktie flapping down his bony bare chest.

Jake took over. "Fred, Bronco—look after the women and our driver. Gus, Jose, and I will take care of this gang, if it comes to that. We're not out to prove anything, so hold back. Fists only. No weapons if we can get away with it. Try not to kill anyone. If we do, it'll make the papers. A few of them are kids; most of them aren't. They're all vicious, but to Americans the sixteen-year-olds are still kids."

"Because they've never been shot by a twelve-year-old with a Winchester," Bronco snapped.

"And we hope to God they never will be," Gus cut in, "which is why we're all here, isn't it?"

Jake's eyes skipped to Gus and Jose, then back to Bronco. "And the kid who shot you went down almost before you did. Three other Rangers shot him."

Though he didn't name names, Elizabeth guessed who two of them were and suspected Jake himself was the third.

His face was tight, expressionless. "Then, it was survival. But not now. The last thing we want is to read in tomorrow's papers that five Frontier Battalion Rangers killed several Mexican kids at a band concert. We'll look bad. Fort Bliss is too important to this country to risk it. None of us wants that."

"The one with the chain tattooed around his neck is no kid," Bronco shot back, his face set and hard. The easygoing Montana cowboy look had vanished.

"I just caught a glint of steel in the streetlight. At least one of these so-called kids has a knife," Gus said. "Curious that only the obvious two kids have Kali sticks. Looks like the older ones won't touch them. If they're soldiers, they know how to use other weapons."

The six Arroyos blended with the others. Now ten hostile men blocked the sidewalk. One made a taunting *come on* gesture with his hands.

Jose took a step forward and spoke quickly in their Mexican Spanish.

He was greeted with hoots and hollers and shouted obscenities in a mixture of Spanish and English.

The kid in the green necktie grabbed the Kali sticks from another boy and moved toward Jose in short little hops. He swung out what looked like shortened broomsticks and started whipping them at Jose.

Instead of moving away, Jose charged, shot his fists

between the whizzing bamboo sticks and yanked them away. In close, he spun and threw his elbow into the kid's face. The young stick fighter squealed and went down, his nose streaming blood over his necktie. Holding his face and whimpering, he crawled away.

"Give me those sticks," Jake demanded, shoving his hand out to the remaining stick fighter.

Big-eyed, the kid dropped the Kali sticks and backed away.

Jake picked them up and turned to Jose. "Let's show them what we do with Kali sticks. You game for a little demonstration?"

Rangers were excellent shots—they all were. Galloping across a field, aiming a Winchester and half standing in the stirrups, they simply didn't miss. Part of their success was familiarity. They knew each other's minds and reactions and what to expect in a crisis. No surprises.

But things were changing. Many times with outlaws and bank robbers, Rangers found themselves fighting in the streets. And when pistols ran out of ammo or a rifle jammed, they had no choice but to defend themselves with their hands. He'd read about different kinds of one-on-one fighting. Such techniques were used to trip or throw the opponent.

Like Filipino stick fighting.

Elizabeth felt the blood drain from her face. "Please, Jake, don't!"

"It's all right. We practice with these. We never know what we'll run into," he said, then looked at the kids, his lip curled in disgust. Sticks up, he advanced toward Jose, who jumped into a fighting stance, one stick across his chest, the other raised.

214

Jake circled, thrust for Jose's throat.

Crack. Stick collided with stick. Jose blocked it.

Jake struck up with the lower end, aiming for Jose's ribs.

Crack. Blocked again.

The street fell strangely silent. In the greenish glow of the streetlight, bamboo Kali sticks whined in the air. Jose let out a high, warbling Navajo scream and lunged at Jake. He swung one of the sticks, whistling down for Jake's head.

Crack.

Another bloodcurdling shriek and a slanting blow aimed at Jake's waist.

Crack.

Every time Jose screamed, Elizabeth flinched. With a sense of dread, she watched, fearing the injury one blow from those sticks could cause. For several minutes, Jake and Jose lashed and struck, almost too fast for the eye to follow.

Crack. Crack. Crack.

The Arroyos cast furtive glances at each other.

At some unspoken signal, Jake and Jose tossed the sticks to Bronco and Fred. Both men snatched them out of the air. From their expressions and how they held the sticks, clearly they also knew how to use them.

Jake spoke, his voice calm. "Jose, tell them to get out of our way."

Suzanne screamed and stumbled.

Chain Man, knife in hand, darted in behind Gus and jerked Suzanne away. Holding the knife at her throat, he yanked her against him. Gus spun around, grabbed for her, and got a fistful of empty air. He caught the tail of her pink sweater instead and whipped it off.

Suzanne fought the man, grabbing at the metal chain around his neck.

Winding the sweater around his forearm, Gus leaped forward and slammed a shoulder into Chain Man, who was trying to escape with Suzanne. Chain Man stumbled, giving Gus a brief opening to snatch away the knife. Gus shot a hand in front of Suzanne's neck and grabbed the man's wrist. Shoving the knife hand high in the air, he shouted at Suzanne to run.

Suzanne twisted and broke away.

As she did, Elizabeth was rushed by two older gang members. Jake had been waiting for them. The first one he stopped cold with a punch to the face and a kick to the ribs; the second one he threw against a building. They both backed away.

Chain Man slashed at Gus repeatedly, but was blocked by the sweater-padded arm. Seizing the man's wrist in a crushing grip, Gus forced him to the ground. The man went down kicking and punching and trying to squirm away. Gus stomped his outstretched leg. With a hoarse scream, the man dropped the knife and collapsed on the sidewalk.

Gus picked up the knife and stared at the rest of the gang.

They also were backing away.

Elizabeth threw her arms around Suzanne and hugged her. Over her shoulder she saw Chain Man writhing on the sidewalk.

Gus turned and put his arms around both women. A moment later he tipped Suzanne's head up. "I'm so sorry," he said.

He glanced back at Chain Man, who was moaning and

holding his leg. "We'll find a doctor after we're out of here," Gus said.

Neither Gus nor Jake was winded. Each man on the team was calm and controlled, as if nothing had happened.

Elizabeth stared at Jake, seeing him in a different light. He'd tried to negotiate around a confrontation, using violence only when forced to. An echo from the past stirred in the back of her mind. Much as she'd loved him, Carl was the opposite. At the first sign of trouble, he would have waded in, fists up.

"Let's finish up here," Jake said. At that moment, his face could have been carved from stone.

Hands flexing, shoulders loose, Jake, Jose, and Gus walked slowly toward the rest of the Arroyos.

The gang members looked at the grim faces of the men approaching them and scattered, yelling, bumping into each other, tripping in their haste to get away. Across the street and down the sidewalk, they ran hard in all directions.

It was over.

Ten minutes later in front of the livery, where Tunnel Street had proper sidewalks, Gus bent down and broke the knife blade in a sidewalk joint. He threw the handle into a trash container and the blade pieces down a sewer.

∞

In the wagon on their way back to Fort Bliss, Suzanne glanced up when Gus slid in beside her. Her palms were damp, and she still felt shaky and scared inside. Not trusting her voice, she turned away and stared off into the distance, her hands clenched together in her lap. Tears were a blink away. Nurses were strong for other people, she told herself. They did not fall apart. She pressed her lips tightly together.

"Hold my hand," Gus whispered. Strong fingers closed around hers.

"I'm not upset anymore." To her chagrin, her voice cracked with strain. She swallowed and forced it under control. "You saved my life tonight, and I'm at a loss how to thank you for that. I'm trying to handle it." She took a deep breath. "I think I'm all right now."

"Well, I'm not. I'm a mess inside. I didn't want you hurt." Gus pried her twisted hands apart and wound his fingers through hers. "What's this?" He pulled a cheap beaded chain from her fingers.

"I don't know. I was holding it when you pulled me away."

He dropped it into his shirt pocket. "It's a chain of some kind. We'll check it out in the light when we get to your house."

Needing to touch him, she gripped his hand in grateful response, then placed her free hand on top of his. She didn't say a word the rest of the way back to the post, just held tight to his big, rough hand with both of hers.

Gus took Suzanne home, while Jake did the same with Elizabeth.

Five minutes after she and Gus walked into her father's house, Suzanne had Gus sitting at her kitchen table, cleaning him up, checking several wounds where the knife had cut him.

Her mother had peeled off his bloody shirt and put it to soak in a pan of soapy water. Leaning against the wall, his arms crossed, her father, Major Peterson, watched silently.

Gus pulled the chain from his pocket. He'd already examined it. "Major," he said, pushing the chain across the tabletop to her father, "do you recognize this?"

Major Peterson held it up to the light and read the metal

tag attached to the chain. *Campo Militar No. 13, Chihuahua.* His mouth tightened. "I recognize it, and so do you, Sergeant. It's Mexican military. Some wear them, some don't. No name, of course. They only put a unit number on the tag." He handed the chain back to Gus. "Colonel Gordon will be most interested. Keep me posted, please. And thank you for protecting our Suzanne tonight."

They chatted for a few minutes longer, and then Suzanne's mother went with her husband to another part of the house.

Gus, his arm outstretched on the tabletop, watched Suzanne, dark eyes wary, tinged with the hardness that Rangers acquired to do what they did. He had a straight Roman nose and a dominant jaw, shadowed and strong.

Though beads of sweat stood out on his forehead as she worked, he made no sound as she cleaned and swabbed the punctures, which she knew were like raw meat inside. Only the involuntary shutting of his eyes revealed when she hurt him. Beneath the desert tan, the skin of his forearm was turning a black and purple color almost as she watched.

She laid the gauze aside and looked up at him. "Let me run you over to the hospital. They can numb your arm for this. At least you won't feel the pain."

"You're doing fine. Doesn't hurt at all."

"Gus, I know better."

He spread a hand over his mouth and wiped his lips. "Just finish and get it over with."

∞

Around midnight, she offered to have a soldier take him home. While the spoonful of laudanum she'd given him had taken the edge off the pain, the way he held his arm against his chest told her it still ached. Being a nurse, she refused to give him any more tonight. Fatigue rimmed his eyes with traces of red.

"You need to get some rest," Suzanne said.

He nodded. "You're right. I am tired." Gus turned from the window, where he'd been checking the front yard for intruders again, and sat down on the couch. Yawning, he kicked off his boots and stretched out.

"That's not what I meant," she said, insisting she wasn't upset from the fight anymore. In the middle of her explanation why he should go home, he rolled over and, as if he'd thrown a switch inside his head, fell fast asleep.

Oh, for heaven's sake. She'd heard Texas Rangers could do that—could go to sleep on command. Until that night, she didn't believe it.

Now what? Hands on her hips, she stood by the couch in her living room. Her gaze rested on the wide tan shoulders, the thick arms. He was in the prime of manhood, strong, healthy. Most women would call him handsome, if you liked the muscled, macho type. A small sigh slipped out. He didn't know it, but she liked *this* one. Very much.

She spread a blanket over him and tucked it around his bare shoulders. "I was so scared," she whispered. "Thank you for not listening to me. I'm glad you're here. My folks want you to come to dinner tomorrow night." Softly so as not to wake him, she stroked his cheek. "So do I."

She turned off the light and went upstairs to bed.

∞

In the dark, Gus smiled.

Twenty-one

CAMPO MILITAR NO. 13
CHIHUAHUA, MEXICO

DIEGO LOOKED UP FROM THE REPORT on his desk, his face angry. "Apparently, if I want a hostage, I'll have to do it myself. Otherwise, mistakes happen. This time, Major, I'm going with you."

"Do you think that's wise, sir?" Major Chavez asked.

Diego pushed himself out of his chair and stared at Chavez. "Probably not, but what's the alternative? Texas Rangers got her away from you in Mexico, and last week the Arroyos themselves backed off from confronting the Rangers. If we plan it right, we can be across the river, grab Elizabeth Evans, and be back in Mexico with her before anyone knows she's gone. I estimate from start to finish, it will take three hours."

EL PASO, TEXAS

"Giddy-yap!" Ruthie called to the horse as she bounced around on Jake's lap.

221

Elizabeth smiled when he slapped the reins and said sternly to the horse, "You heard the little lady."

As usual, Jake was within reaching distance. Until things quieted down across the border, her father wanted her accompanied wherever she went, and Colonel Gordon had agreed.

During the day, Jake—if he was free, or a soldier from Fort Bliss if he wasn't—escorted her wherever she needed to go and dropped her off. For the next few months, she was never to be out in public without security.

Ruthie lifted her face and gave Jake a loud, damp kiss on the cheek.

He laughed. "Why don't you teach your aunt to do that?"

The buggy moved away from Elizabeth's quarters and headed past the well-groomed flower beds for the road through the post. Once through the main gate, it was an easy three miles to El Paso.

Ruthie sat on Jake's lap, holding his hands with the reins and pretending she was driving the horse herself. Elizabeth spent as much time with her as possible, and so did Jake.

That afternoon, Elizabeth was going into the newspaper office to say hello to everyone and see what she could do to help. She didn't know many people in town yet, but a few neighbors recognized her in the buggy and called to her. Pleased, she waved back. Jake pulled over and let her out to talk to two women.

When she climbed in again, he drove back out into the street. She smiled at him. "That was thoughtful. Thanks. I hardly know anyone yet."

"You've got a lot ahead of you," he said.

On the wooden sidewalk outside the newspaper office,

she held Ruthie's hand and read the sign running across the building: THE GRANDE EXAMINER. Sadness welled up that Lloyd wasn't here to see it with her. Jake, watching her, said nothing, though he moved closer.

"I'll never be able to take his place," she said.

Jake took her hand. "I think he'd tell you not to try." He was quiet for several moments and then spoke hesitantly, as though he had to pull the words out.

"You haven't talked about it, but I don't think he'd want you and Ruthie decked out in black because something happened to him. We talked once about it—he called it morbid. He told me how your father dressed you and him in black after your mother died, and he said your father wept every time he did it. You were six years old."

Jake let out a deep breath. "I'm sorry if I'm saying something you don't want to hear. It's just that since he felt strongly about it, I thought you should know."

"And you?" she asked. "How do you feel?"

"I think grief is private. How you handle it is your decision."

Elizabeth straightened. "I've heard my father make reference to it, but he was a young congressman then in Washington, which has a rigid society. He had to conform or he'd have found himself an outcast. That's not the case out here. We're on the frontier, and that eases a lot of the restrictions. I didn't realize Lloyd felt the same."

The sadness left as she stepped through the door. Two of the writers jumped to their feet. "Here's our celebrity back from Mexico. We're so glad you're back," Ezra Stuart said, a balding man with glasses.

When she started to introduce Jake, Ezra grabbed his

hand and shook it. "We all know Jake. Lloyd brought him in several times."

Ezra introduced her to two workers she hadn't met before. One of them asked, "What can we do to help you get started?"

Elizabeth threw her hands out. "Everything."

She greeted each of them, trying to learn a bit about them, and who did what at the newspaper.

"I've been thinking and need your input on a lot of things. How about El Paso schools? There's only one and it's not open all the time. How about we campaign for more public schools for the children? We have ten thousand people now and desperately need more schools."

She looked up, shaking her head. "And law enforcement. In the last eight months, I understand we've had six sheriffs. That's a serious problem. Our police department needs more structure and tighter rules. And more officers."

Ezra Stuart stared at her and clapped his hands. "Welcome home, and thank you, Elizabeth Madison Evans. You are certainly your brother's sister."

A rush of embarrassment warmed her cheeks. "I have a lot to learn, so you'll have to lead me like a little child. Lloyd always talked about efficiency and saving the reporters' time. I probably don't know how to do that yet, but we can get someone in here who does. We want the *Grande Examiner* to be the best newspaper in West Texas!"

Everyone cheered and clapped their hands.

Ruthie did the same, jumping up and down and clapping her hands. Jake smiled, shook his head, and took her next door for ice cream.

Elizabeth followed Ezra through the long narrow room

and into a small corner office with glass sides reaching halfway to the ceiling. Lloyd's office. Her office now, she reminded herself.

It was also their telegraph office. When the key started clicking, receiving a message, a buzzer went off in the main office. This was how they got the latest news from other parts of the country.

A counter ran the length of one wall. On it sat typewriters and a typesetting machine, with a printing press set up at its end. A large table with rollers and heavy mats had been placed in the center of the room.

Elizabeth grinned when a telephone jangled two short and one long ring. Lloyd, open to new inventions, had insisted on telephones as soon as they were available. She saw several in the office. He didn't want his reporters having to chase down some fact in a story that could be verified by telephone. As a result, the stories in the *Examiner* came together quicker.

Before she finished at the newspaper office, she called everyone together and asked them for suggestions on an edition about Mexico—everything from political instability and the threats of General Diego to forging better relations between Juarez on one side of the Rio Grande and El Paso on the other.

"What would you think if we hired a Mexican reporter from Juarez?" she asked.

The surprised stares on the men's faces changed to approval and chuckles.

Ezra rubbed his hands together. "How about a column in the *Examiner* inviting applications?"

"Perfect, Ezra. Let's do that. And when the time comes to choose, we will decide together," she said.

"You know, I was worried about the paper with Lloyd gone," Ezra said. "I'm not anymore. We're going to be just fine."

"Shhh, stop kicking me," a deep voice said in the outer office. "Your aunt is busy now. She'll be out in a minute."

"Aunt 'Lithabeth, Aunt 'Lithabeth, I want in there with you. Make him put me down!" Ruthie called.

Elizabeth laughed and stood up. "Gentlemen, I must go for now. I think one Texas Ranger has finally met his match."

Twenty-two

CAMP ANNEX

JAKE YAWNED AND RUBBED HIS FACE with both hands, rasping the bristles on his jaw. He still wasn't caught up. His desk was littered with papers: Ranger evaluations, schedules, weekly reports.

Six hours in a saddle didn't faze him, but six hours at a desk kinked every muscle he had. He leaned back in his chair and rolled his shoulders to loosen them.

And ferrying Elizabeth around—when she so obviously thought it unnecessary—didn't help any. But her father had explained the situation to her. She argued with Jake, but she didn't argue with him.

"Like it or not, this man," her father had said, pointing to Jake, "is your bodyguard. Those are my wishes, Elizabeth. And fortunately, he and Colonel Gordon concur. When Jake isn't available, someone else will take his place. It's not permanent, so do what you can to help these men keep you alive."

Taking her into town this afternoon had gone well. She hadn't protested once. Either Jake was doing something right or Elizabeth was simply getting used to it.

Or figuring out ways to get around all of them and do as she pleased.

No, that wasn't fair to her. She'd deal with it, and deal with him, up front.

Even though the Army and the Rangers considered it work, he liked spending time with her. A couple of mornings when she needed to finish up an article for the paper, like the one on military medicine, he and Gus took her to the hospital for breakfast with Suzanne.

Gus had added a personal touch to that article, and Elizabeth included his remarks that Fort Bliss was fortunate to have a good Army surgeon and dedicated nurses on staff. That article was forwarded by Colonel Gordon to Army headquarters.

At a light tapping on the door, he raised his head and called, "Come in."

When the door opened, he smiled and sprang to his feet. Hand outstretched, he crossed the room quickly and greeted his Gypsy friend Laszlo.

"Any trouble getting here?" Jake asked.

Laszlo shook his head. "Only problem was getting past the guard at the entrance. And still he followed me right to your door."

Jake pulled up a chair for Laszlo, then sat and faced him.

"Remember when I told you Gypsies have ways of finding things out?" Laszlo said.

"I remember very well, and I'm listening."

"I knew you would, which is why I came." Laszlo leaned

forward, his eyes locked with Jake's. "Diego is coming after our Hoopa lady."

Jake dragged a hand down his face and rose from his chair. "From the day we got back, I've been afraid of that." Standing by his desk, he looked at Laszlo. "How did you find this out?"

"One of my people cleans Diego's office."

"And?"

"He hears things."

"What else?"

"There's an old Gypsy saying that goes, 'A little wine goes in, a little truth comes out.'"

Jake nodded. "I've heard that. What came out?"

"That Diego is getting very close to overthrowing Hector Guevara. However, he needs an angry response from the United States. He thinks taking Elizabeth again will bring that about. He also intends to increase the guerrilla attacks on Texas ranchers. Right now he's at his camp, but I know where he goes to hide, if you want to go after him."

"If I could, I'd go tonight, but that's a decision someone in my government has to make. I can't just ride into Mexico and kidnap one of their generals and put him on trial. He'll swear he's innocent, deny everything. And the next thing I know, he's free, and I'm in jail. As a result, Mexico and the United States would be at each other's throats again." Jake leaned forward. "It's getting too late for you to start back. You had anything to eat lately?"

Laszlo shook his head. "Not since breakfast this morning. I was in a hurry."

"Let's go over to the fort. We'll have a quick supper, and afterward we'll share your information with some people

I know. You've got contacts in Mexico that just might be useful to them."

He owed this man. Laszlo had taken a big risk to get them out of Mexico and back to Texas. And now he'd come on his own to Texas to warn him of a threat to Elizabeth.

"We have plenty of beds here at the Annex. Later, you're welcome to stay the night with us."

Laszlo's dark eyes lit up. "You mean it? Here, in the Ranger camp?"

Jake nodded.

Laszlo smiled. "I'd like that very much. You make this poor Gypsy feel important."

Laszlo *was* important. He had no idea how important.

"Let's go eat," Jake said.

⌒

The Officers' Club was on a side street, down two doors from the commissary, and well away from the living quarters for both officers and the men.

"How about a drink first?" Jake said, sliding onto a high-backed stool at the bar. "A sarsaparilla for me," he said to the bartender.

Laszlo nodded at the bartender. "I'll have a beer."

Through the double doors leading from the bar to the dining room, Jake watched officers and their families lining up at the buffet table for Beef and Beer Night. Though the food was casual, fresh flowers and white tablecloths were the order of the day. Pride and a certain elegance was unmistakable. Even the greeter at the door wore a suit and tie, and bowed as the officers entered.

Officers were treated with formal respect, almost a

requirement, especially for those forts far out in the back-country. It was intended as a reminder of the privileges U.S. Army officers were entitled to—no matter where they were or how lonely the post in which they found themselves.

"Thanks," Jake said as the bartender slid the mugs in front of them. They carried their drinks to a table by the window, then went into the dining room to the buffet table to get their food.

Back at their table, Jake looked up at Laszlo and said, "Elizabeth asked me to find someone who could fix her house, repair the damage so she can move back in. How are you at work like that?"

"I built my own vardo," Laszlo said.

"Nice work. I'm impressed. So I can tell her you'd be interested in the job?"

"I'd be interested in any job," Laszlo replied. His eyes filled and he looked away quickly.

"Good," Jake said with a smile. "This week we'll go out to the house and see what all needs to be done." His expression then turned serious. "Now let's go talk to Colonel Gordon and see what he wants us to do about Diego."

Twenty-three

THE NEXT DAY, ON A NARROW STRIP OF BEACH on the Mexican shore, Major Chavez and General Diego, both wearing civilian clothes, walked their horses into the Rio Grande near Socorro, downstream from El Paso.

Diego, an excellent horseman, led the way across.

Chavez followed, chafing at his position. He should have been leading, not Diego. Chavez knew the route; the general did not. He swallowed his irritation, knowing full well that generals don't like following lowly majors.

When they'd reached the other side, Diego looked for an easy way up the riverbank to the road.

"Which way, Major?" Diego asked.

Chavez smiled. "Follow me, General," he said, pulling around Diego and starting up an incline so steep, his horse lunged like a mountain goat. At the edge of a road at the top, he looked down at the general. Diego nodded, kicked his horse hard, and leaped up the bank to the top.

Looking around, Diego said in disgust, "More sand. So, how far to El Paso?"

"Fifteen miles maybe," Chavez said. "This is called the

Old Road. It's not as good as the new one, lots of deep ruts, but it has advantages. Few people use it, so we won't be noticed. And if we stay on it, we can miss El Paso completely and ride on to Lloyd Madison's house."

"And how far is Madison's from El Paso?" Diego asked.

"Three miles, no more," Chavez answered.

General Diego nodded.

"We're wasting time," he said. "Let's head out." Then he gave his horse another powerful kick.

Twenty-four

EL PASO

"THIS IS IT." Elizabeth leaned forward and pointed to a white house with black shutters, set well back off the road and overlooking the juncture of the Rio Grande and, upstream, the bubbling rapids where the Little Pine Creek flowed in.

Jake turned the buggy through the main gate and drove up the lane to C. E. Kaufman's house.

Kaufman, a prominent attorney in town, had offered his home and grounds to the Wesley Women's Society, which was sponsoring a town picnic that included educating the women about weapons.

Jake glanced at the paper in Elizabeth's lap.

The headline read, *Texas Rangers Teach El Paso Women to Shoot*. Elizabeth had run two articles on it, giving the time and date of the picnic. Men were invited to the picnic, but the lesson on weapons afterward was for women only, the article said, offered for their and their families' protection.

"Good advertising for the paper as well as your picnic," Jake said. He chuckled. "Still don't understand how you talked Kaufman into this gun picnic idea."

"Shhh, don't call it that. I met him in church. You were with me the day he and his wife introduced themselves, remember?"

Jake nodded. "Don't remember you asking him to do this, though."

"I didn't then. His wife stopped by the paper the next week, and I suggested it." The buggy went over a rut then, and she bounced up and down in the seat. "I'm so excited. I hope it goes well."

People were coming from every direction—ranch wives, farm wives, women who felt vulnerable when they were alone. A few who lived in town came, well-dressed women wearing gloves and big hats.

Out on the road, a line of wagons, buggies, and men on horseback waited to turn in through the gate.

Sergeant Gus Dukker in a purple- and yellow-striped shirt manned the gate, directing the drivers to park in a field at the other end of the picnic area. Being a Ranger, with a gun on each hip, he was also checking the occupants of each buggy or wagon to make sure no troublemakers showed up.

The grounds had been decorated with red, white, and blue streamers and hand-lettered signs. Balloons were tied to every table and handed out to the children. From the far side of the grounds came shouts of laughter. A blue haze rose when another string of firecrackers went off.

"The people of El Paso have done everything right," Jake said to Elizabeth. "To someone passing by, it looks like a town picnic."

"Which it is," she said.

"But with a difference. There's more weaponry at this picnic today than in some entire towns."

Sheriff Bud Wagner, his wounded leg propped on a bench, sat with Deputy Morgan at a table laid out with guns under a sign that said, *Law Enforcement.*

Women in long white aprons worked at a yard-long griddle borrowed from a local restaurant and hung over a wood fire. Sausages and Red Hots sizzled.

Next to the griddle, a side of beef turned in a huge fire pit. Peppery steam swirled and rose from it, stinging their eyes. From time to time, Reverend Sam Lewis painted it with more hot sauce.

The old national flag of what used to be the Republic of Texas—red, white, and blue with a single star—fluttered proudly alongside the Stars and Stripes.

Jake pulled up with the buggy, helped Elizabeth down, and unloaded boxes of rifles and ammunition. Six Rangers from D Company rode in right behind them. They tied up their horses and Jake's buggy and came back to get the teachers' tables set up. Each table displayed an assortment of rifles and pistols. Rangers would demonstrate care and handling of the different types of weapons. Out in the field behind a barn, paper targets had been set in a line.

One table was already surrounded by ladies and girls, all of them smiling at the young officer in the dark blue Cavalry coat and sky blue trousers so familiar on the frontier. The broad yellow stripe down each trouser leg announced his officer status, as did the wide-brimmed black campaign hat trimmed with gold and tipped up at the side.

Lieutenant Mark Taylor, the officer who had brought the

telegram to Jake the day Elizabeth was kidnapped, waved to Jake as he passed.

Jake came over and nodded at the girls gathered around the table. "Glad you came in uniform," he said to the lieutenant. "It shows everyone how neighborly El Paso and Fort Bliss are." He smiled, lowered his voice and added, "And the ladies seem to love that uniform."

Ignoring Jake's comment, Lieutenant Taylor said, "As you can see, I brought a Springfield military rifle and two Army Colts for my demonstration. By the way, thanks for asking for me. My captain was very impressed." He grinned. "That pretty lady with you a minute ago—at the next table—is that Elizabeth Evans?"

Jake turned, glanced at Elizabeth, who was talking and laughing with one of his Rangers. "That's her," he said.

"No wonder you were so determined to get her back."

Jake laughed, clapped Taylor on the shoulder. "And I'm going to keep her away from you in that uniform."

"Anyone with property to protect, over here, please," a Ranger called. Behind him, the deputy sheriff had set up a blackboard. People crowded around. The Ranger and the sheriff drew roads in and out of El Paso and sketched in the Rio Grande for reference. They circled properties that might be at risk.

At one of the Ranger tables, Fred Barkley stripped a rifle. In half a minute he'd taken the weapon completely apart. Next, he took out the firing pin, the spring, all while explaining what each piece did. Then, just as quickly, he put the pieces back together. The women gathered around, listening to him describe each step.

He showed a woman how to hold the rifle, get comfortable

with it, then pass it along to the woman next to her. After everyone had a chance to hold the gun and sight it, then came the actual shooting at targets. A Ranger stood behind each woman taking a turn, holding her left elbow and guiding the rifle against her shoulder.

"Why that's not hard at all!" one said, lining up for a second turn.

Confident and smiling, some of them sought out Elizabeth, who was standing in the next line for her third chance with a Winchester Model 1886.

The afternoon flew by. Finally, Jake cast an anxious look at the setting sun and called an end to the target practice.

Over the groans and pleas to shoot a while longer, he said, "For shooting, you need good light. Remember, ladies—always think safety."

Twenty-five

IT WAS LATE AFTERNOON when Chavez and the general turned into the lane leading to Madison's house. Chavez took him up to the barn first, which was dark and empty inside. No horses; they'd been hauled away. No chickens and no dogs, for they'd been disposed of, also.

"All the curtains are pulled. The place looks deserted," Diego said, riding back to the house. "Was it like this when you were here?"

"Not at all. I just assumed the woman was still living here. There was also a child and a housekeeper. Now, no one."

Frowning, Diego walked up the steps to the front door. Locked.

He threw his shoulder against it several times until finally the lock gave way and the door swung open.

They stepped inside and looked around.

"What happened in here?" Diego asked.

"When my men saw that Lloyd Madison was gone, they got all angry. And this"—Chavez swept his hand at the overturned furniture and broken lamps—"was the result of that."

241

"This is why the Evans woman left. Thanks to your men, the place is almost unlivable." Diego smacked his hand against the wall and swore. "Why didn't you tell me what we'd find before we came all the way out here?" He snapped his head up. "I don't suppose you know where Elizabeth Evans lives now?"

Chavez's eyes grew wide and he shook his head.

"I didn't think so," Diego said, and stormed out the door and down the front steps. He mounted his horse and started down the lane for the road back to Socorro.

∞

Whistling under his breath, Laszlo headed down the Old Road for the cutoff to El Paso. Strange . . . The two riders a quarter mile ahead weren't there a minute ago. He looked around. He'd passed no houses and no roads for the last mile. There were none except the lane he was coming up on, the driveway to the Hoopa Lady's house. He'd ridden into town with Jake and Elizabeth this morning to help unload chairs for the weapons demonstration this afternoon. Jake pointed out her house as they went by.

On impulse, he turned into the lane and trotted up to the house. Quiet. Everything seemed all right.

Not quite.

The front door stood wide open.

Laszlo didn't get off his horse. Instead, he turned him around and took off at a gallop back to the Old Road. As he came up behind the two men, he noticed the saddles—Mexican military saddles. And he'd seen both of the men before, but in Mexican uniforms.

Chavez and Diego.

Bad news for the Hoopa Lady.

He took the road along the river through El Paso and out to the picnic, where he swung off his horse to look for Jake and Elizabeth.

"Jake! Jake!" he called, waving his arms over his head.

Jake hurried over. "What's wrong?"

"I just saw him!" Laszlo said, breathless. "He's here. Diego's *here!*"

Twenty-six

"WE'RE GOING TO ARREST THEM," Jake said.

He talked quietly to six Rangers, the sheriff and his deputy, all circled around the Law Enforcement table. Every man was wearing guns.

Gus shook his head. "Diego and Chavez may just show up here. They think no one knows them. They're wearing civilian clothes, and both speak English. Even if they didn't speak English, it wouldn't be noticed in El Paso. More people speak Spanish than English here, anyway."

Gus clapped a hand on Laszlo's shoulder. "My friend here says the general is without his usual mustache. Major Chavez has a scarred right cheek. Let's spread out, and keep our eyes open. Any doubts, spread the word to Fred or me. Not Jake; they know Jake. But as far as we know, they don't know us."

Wide-eyed, Elizabeth pulled at Jake's arm. "Surely they wouldn't come here."

"They might. But don't worry—we'll be ready for them." Jake turned to Laszlo. "Take Elizabeth someplace safe and keep her out of sight."

"Where can we go, Hoopa Lady?" Laszlo asked, leading her aside.

Elizabeth looked around and shrugged. "Not inside the Kaufman house. There are children in there."

"There's no place else around here, except for maybe the barn," Laszlo said.

"The barn's too close to other people. Those men have guns." Her lips pursed. "The woods . . . I see lots of big trees and bushes."

"Or we could go back to the Annex. There are Rangers there."

"And meet the Mexicans on the way? Not on your life," Elizabeth said.

☙

Moments later, Diego and Chavez rode up the long driveway of the Kaufman house.

Gus, the official greeter, welcomed them, gave each a balloon and a small Texas flag. Other than himself, there wasn't a Ranger in sight.

A drum roll sounded. The leader chinned his fiddle and called, "Yee-HAW! Grab your lady, here we go. Grab her now, boys, and do-si-do."

Gus said, "You're just in time for the dance, gentlemen."

Under a yellow awning next to the barn, the Franklin Mountain Boys, in boots and Stetsons, led into a fast hoe-down.

Gus pointed to the trees that lined the side of the big yard. "Tie your horses over there, and enjoy the music."

The two men looked at each other, nodded, then swung down and began leading their horses toward the trees.

"Look around. Do you see the Evans woman?" Diego asked Chavez.

"No. Not yet."

As they approached the trees, Diego glanced back at Gus and wrinkled his forehead. "I'm sure I've seen that man before. Recently. In Mexico."

Chavez looked back. "Let's leave, then. If you're right, they know us, and won't let us out the way we came in. I know this area. The woods end at a creek that empties into the Rio Grande, but there's a drop-off and the water's too deep. We have to follow it upstream and cross where it's shallow, then find the Grande on that side."

Diego got back on his horse and rode slowly into the trees, as if looking for a place to tie the horse. Chavez was right behind him. When they were well into the woods, they kicked their horses into a run.

∞

A shot whistled overhead, tearing through the leaves, followed by another. Jake, hidden until now, ran from tree to tree, chasing them through the woods, firing above their heads. He didn't want to kill them. The government needed them alive for prosecution, not only in the United States but in Mexico, too.

Dodging the trees, Diego headed for the drop-off to the creek up ahead. As they drew nearer to the creek, they slowed, looking for some way across. There, the creek was deep and wide with steep banks.

Jake jumped out from behind a tree and dragged Diego off his horse. Diego swore and swung at him. On the way down, Diego fumbled for his pistol, but dropped it as he yanked it out.

Jake punched him in the face—a short, hard jab. Diego's head snapped to the side. Jake pulled back to hit him again.

From behind, hard steel struck the back of Jake's head and buckled his knees. A red burst of fire and pain exploded behind his eyes. He knew it was a pistol butt from the way it felt.

The world tilted. The sky swirled, a blur of clouds and treetops. Slowly he fell onto his face.

"Get back on your horse, General," he heard Chavez say, the words sounding distant.

"After I kill him."

"No! A shot will give us away. We'll come back later, and you can finish him off then."

"Don't you give me orders. I'll do as I please." Then, cursing and rubbing his jaw, Diego mounted up, and the two rode off.

Hearing them leave, Jake moaned, struggled to move.

∞

On her stomach under a thick, scratchy bush, Elizabeth put a finger over Laszlo's lips. She placed her mouth against his ear. "Go get the others," she said.

Laszlo pushed himself out backward, then ran for the clearing.

Elizabeth rushed over to Jake. "Lie still. Let me see what's wrong."

He looked up into her eyes. Elizabeth, her arm around his shoulders, bent over him with a concerned frown.

"Don't look so worried, darlin'. I'll live." His broad Texas accent thickened, dragged out as slow as sorghum. "I'll be all right."

But the skin around his eyes tightened as he winced in pain. He clenched his teeth, and then his face relaxed, his eyes glazed over and he passed out.

She went down on her knees beside him. He lay deathly still, his face the color of chalk. The back of his head was bleeding and a knot was growing. He was big, heavy, and out cold. She jerked her head up at a noise in the trees, and the stumble of her heartbeat raced in her ears. They were coming back to kill him. Her too.

Her mind jumped from one idea to another. Think! Think! They were close to the top of the high bank, maybe six feet above the water.

She stretched his arms down straight at his sides and pulled and tugged until he was at the brink. She looked at the creek below. Farther than she'd realized. She put one hand on his belt, the other on his shoulders.

"Sorry, Jake," she said, then pushed him over the edge.

Like a log, he rolled down the bank, gaining momentum until he splashed into the creek. And sank.

He wasn't supposed to sink!

She grabbed up her skirt and leaped, landing hard on her backside, and slid the rest of the way down, her skirt riding halfway to her middle.

She jumped into the creek and dove down, following the air bubbles. She found an arm, pushed off the bottom and shot for the surface, pulling him up with her. When his head broke the surface, his eyes were still closed.

Creek water poured down his face.

Bobbing beside him, she fished a foot down, feeling for the bottom. The creek was surprisingly deep and cold. Holding Jake, she pushed away from the bank and looked for a place to hide. A short distance away was a tall patch of bulrushes.

"Good enough for Moses, good enough for you," she muttered to him.

Both of them would be hidden and out of sight, especially with night coming. But big as he was and completely dressed, he was weighing her down. Her wet skirt had tangled around her legs. She had to push to keep her own face out of the water.

With hardly a ripple she rolled onto her side, her left arm around his chest, towing him, and keeping that blond head of his out of the water.

He groaned a deep, breathy sound she could feel in his chest.

"It's all right, Jake. Stop squirming. I've got you. Don't fight me or we'll both go down."

"God . . . help me," he whispered, as though just realizing where he was. He raised his chin, panic in his eyes.

Quickly so as not to tip off the Mexicans, she lowered her face and kissed him full on the mouth, shutting off any sound from him. Under her mouth, his eyes opened wide.

She slid her mouth sideways a fraction. "Shhh, they're back. I hear them up there. Don't make a sound. If they find us, they'll kill us both. Understand me?"

He nodded. "Yes, but—"

Her mouth covered his again.

She bent the stiff green stalks aside and peered through, swimming and working deeper into the rushes. She shifted Jake around in her arms and hugged him tight, wondering if he was going to die and how she could live with herself if he did.

She fisted a handful of rushes and wrapped a leg around the stalks, floating upright in the water and holding Jake against her. He couldn't reach bottom, either. The creek was over their heads.

Her breath caught when shots rang out, followed by curses and shouts coming from the top of the bank.

A loud, deep voice yelled, "Hold it right there, General. One move and you're dead. Under the laws of the state of Texas, you are under arrest."

It was Gus! *Thank you, God.*

"Gus!" she called. "Jake's down here in the creek with me. Please, help us. Jake is hurt."

There was a long pause. "I don't see you."

"Off to your right, in the creek. Hold on a minute. We'll swim out so you can see us."

"Jake can't swim."

She made a face. "I know that now."

"If I throw you a rope, can you tie it under his arms?"

"Yes. But hurry. He needs a doctor."

∽

As soon as the men hauled her up the bank, she ran to Jake and fell on her knees beside him, feeling his throat for a pulse. He'd passed out again. She stood and looked at the men. "He's unconscious. Get a wagon and take him to Fort Bliss. And please hurry."

The Rangers had General Diego and Major Chavez handcuffed, legs bound. Three Rangers held Colts on them.

Both the sheriff and his deputy were there, getting ready to take the prisoners to the jail in El Paso.

Gus approached the sheriff. "These men are accused of

both state and Federal crimes, Sheriff," he said. "The last thing this town needs is a company of angry Mexican troops invading to reclaim their general. I think everyone would feel safer—you included—if we get these men out of El Paso at once. Until we get the jurisdictions settled, they belong in the stockade at Fort Bliss."

Twenty-seven

GLASS JINGLED BEHIND HER. Elizabeth spun around. An Army medic, wheeling a rubber-tired cart past the Fort Bliss Emergency Room, met her startled look with a sympathetic smile. Elizabeth swallowed. The smell of disinfectant clung in the back of her throat. She hated hospitals, needles, the hushed voices. And the white silence turned her insides to jelly.

She slumped onto the bench again with Gus and Fred. Time and again, they got up and walked with her when she went outside and stood under the portico of the large masonry building. She looked up and down the street that led to the parade grounds at the end of the block.

"Relax," Gus said. "There's nothing to worry about. Jake's safe. You're safe. There are guards at the gate, and sentries patrol everywhere else. No one gets onto this post without permission."

A young doctor in a white surgical coat sat down beside her. "Captain Nelson has been examined and is resting now in a room upstairs. He has a deep cut on the back of his head, and as near as we can tell, he's suffered a concussion. We're going to keep him here and observe him for a few days. Just a precaution. He should be fine in a week or so."

He smiled and patted her shoulder. "He's in Room 224. Go on upstairs and see him."

Elizabeth got to her feet.

"Doctor, I'm soaked. We jumped into the creek to get away. Can I possibly borrow something dry until tomorrow?" When he hesitated, she added, "I'm Elizabeth Evans, Senator Madison's daughter. My father and I are living temporarily on post. I'll see they're laundered and returned to the hospital tomorrow."

"Of course. I'll let someone know right away."

Elizabeth blew out a breath, relieved. She intended to stay in Jake's room. She asked no one. She simply went.

Usually she never mentioned her father, but this time his name and position helped. If necessary, she'd throw it around. She intended to stay in Jake's room all night, and if they didn't like it, well, she'd deal with that when it came up.

"I'm going to sit in his room with him," she said to the doctor and Gus.

Gus nodded. "And I'll sit outside the door."

"I thought you told me a minute ago there was nothing to worry about."

"I intend to make sure of it."

Elizabeth didn't want Jake waking up alone in a strange place. Bad enough to have a cracked head. He didn't need to worry about where he was in the middle of the night.

∞

Jake spread a hand across the back of his head and frowned. Bandaged. A deep, dull pain shoved at the back of his eyes. He was in a high, narrow bed with metal sides.

A hospital?

Slowly he turned his head toward the only light in the room—a wall lamp, the gas turned down low.

Barefooted, wearing a pair of baggy Army trousers and a khaki shirt, Elizabeth was dozing in a chair in the corner, her legs drawn up under her. Her dark hair had fallen over one cheek, giving her an innocent, girlish look. Lifting her head, she got out of the chair and hurried over to the bed.

Bits and pieces came back to him: the fight with Diego, getting struck from behind, then rolling out of control down the creek bank. And cold water filling his ears, his nose. He shuddered. He'd never forget that feeling. Never.

"You pushed me into the water," he whispered.

She smiled down at him. "You remember that, do you?"

"But not much more . . . How did I get here?"

"In a caravan of noisy wagons, with half of El Paso's horses and buggies trailing behind. It was an interesting ride. Now go back to sleep."

He glanced at Elizabeth again. She'd kissed him in the water to shut him up—like a soft punch in the mouth. Nothing romantic about that kiss. The more he thought about it, the more he didn't like it.

As if she read his mind, she leaned down and kissed him softly on the lips.

"See you in the morning," she said.

"That's better," he said, sighing and closing his eyes. A gray fog folded around him and he drifted off to sleep, happy to be watched over.

∽

For the next two weeks, his Rangers and Elizabeth made Jake take it easy. Since he couldn't do much else, she insisted that he, and any other non-swimming Ranger, learn how to swim.

Reluctantly he gave in, but only after dragging four of his ten-man Ranger crew out to the water with him.

"I'll help you," Gus said to one of the men, striding around the little pond at the far end of Fort Bliss. It wasn't over anyone's head except in the middle.

Elizabeth had found a swimming outfit in town, ugly to be sure, but at least she could swim in it. It had bloomers down below her knees, stockings, and a long ruffled tunic over it.

The men swam in simple trousers and a shirt.

The first day, Elizabeth showed them breathing positions and how to move their arms. Five large, well-muscled men stepped into the pond and did the swimming exercises, silent and sullen at first. But soon their embarrassment wore off.

The next day, she and Gus each took a learner deeper into the pond and made him lie on the water. Gus held them up while Elizabeth coached them about how to relax.

Watching from the bank, Jake called out encouragement. "Hey, listen to her. She knows what she's talking about. I'm here to prove it."

By the end of the week, almost all of the men were getting the hang of it, learning well the basic strokes. Elizabeth, pleased by their progress, let them know they were now swimmers. Together they clapped to their success.

"It seems they have lost their fear of it," Elizabeth announced that evening to Jake. To celebrate the fact, she had a little party at her house for everyone.

Jake, she thought, was hopeless. He was one of those heavy-boned men who did not float easily. He sank.

Twenty-eight

THE FORT'S SMALL TWO-SEATER BUGGY Jake had access to was waiting out front when Elizabeth left the newspaper office the following evening. If he wasn't tied up with work, he always came for her. If he couldn't get away, he sent another Ranger in his place.

When he saw her coming, a smile broke out across his face. He put away the paper he was reading, reached for her hand, and helped her into the buggy.

"How'd it go today?" he asked.

"Gets better all the time. People are giving me items for the paper. The Presbyterian minister even stopped by and gave me a list of the Women's Benevolence Club meetings. Someday I'll write a piece about it."

She smoothed her blue-striped skirt over her knees and looked up. "He said we have three fatherless families in town. I didn't know that."

"Neither did I," Jake said. "The number's gone up. I knew about two. Every week there's a fight or a shooting in town. We need a bigger jail. The sheriff is short on men and jail space. He's county. We need a city police force. The less serious ones, he lets out on bail—has to—until their court dates come up. He only jails a shooter if it's a killing. Otherwise, bail or no bail, they take off."

"Lloyd once said the town is growing too fast."

"He was right about that, but how do you slow it down? And why would you want to? El Paso has a great future ahead of it. That's why they put us here. Ordinarily Rangers go in only when there's trouble. But I've got Rangers walking El Paso streets as a deterrent. Bad enough with our homegrown outlaws, but Mexican crimes are increasing all the time. Bandits pour over the border and steal whatever they get their hands on. Mexico's trying to help, but we have to get tougher ourselves."

Elizabeth's eyebrows drew together. El Paso was up to ten thousand people now, ninety percent of them having arrived in the last two years. They came with the four railroads. Opportunities for everyone, thieves and outlaws included. Jake didn't want her out on the street after dark.

He flicked the reins, urging the horse faster. "It's worse than you think," he said. "There are saloons and gambling parlors on every street. Every street! Town needs a proper police force."

"Maybe you should talk to the city council."

"I'm thinking about it."

She twisted around in her seat. "While you're thinking about it, think about stopping by Bailey's General Store on our way back to the fort, and I'll set up a time to talk to Tim Bailey. His wife came into my office today to tell me about some new butter thing with peanuts that people are going giddy over in Austin and back East. She thinks it'll make a great article for the new Homemaker Hints page I'm running in the women's section." Elizabeth laughed. "Of course, Tim Bailey is going to stock it, so it's good advertising for him."

Bailey's, one of the largest and most prosperous stores in El Paso, was located farther down Main Street than most of the other shops. It was a stand-alone building with lots of buggy space on each side.

Jake pulled up to the store, then jumped down and walked around to help Elizabeth out of the buggy.

Elizabeth looked up at him. "This morning, you said your icebox had three eggs, two biscuits, and a bottle of milk in it."

"Which is why I took you and Ruthie out for breakfast."

She gave an unladylike sniff. "Sure, to the post cafeteria—and I paid."

He laughed. "I told you. I forgot my wallet."

At the entrance, he braced the front door open with his shoulder for her and then followed her into the store, past a large pyramid display of canned fruits and vegetables.

Jake chuckled. "Tomorrow I promise I'll go shop for food. . . ." His voice trailed off.

Behind the counter, a white-faced Tim Bailey scooped a handful of bills from the register. Eyes wide, he pushed the money across the counter to a customer, a bearlike man with his back to the door. At the sound of voices, the huge man spun around.

Gun!

Jake exploded into a blur, racing for the counter. A jump, a flying kick, and the pistol was shoved upward an instant before flame burst from its muzzle. The glass in the front door they'd entered just seconds before blew out from the shot. A second shot hit the display of canned tomatoes, showering red pulp everywhere.

Elizabeth screamed. The display toppled to the floor, cans rolling in every direction.

The heavy pistol hit the floor and slid down the dry goods aisle. The gunman lunged at Jake, who twisted out of the way just in time. Jake ran to a nearby rack of spades and shovels, grabbed one, swung around and struck the man across the face as he was about to throw a fist. The man went down with a thud.

Jake stood over him, the shovel ready for another blow. "Elizabeth, are you all right?"

"I think so, Jake . . . yes."

A quick glance confirmed it—she *was* all right. Jake let out a sigh of relief.

Flat on his back and dazed, the big man rose up on one elbow. Blood dribbled from his mouth. "You busted my jaw," he muttered, the words slurred.

Jake had held back because Elizabeth was there. She looked stunned by the scene before her. The last thing he wanted was for her to see him kill someone. He regretted she'd seen him do this much. But if one of those shots had hit her . . . He threw down the shovel.

The man turned his head and spat blood. "I'll kill you for this, mister. I don't care who you are. I'll kill you."

Jake jumped on the man then, slammed his face against the wood floor. He leaned down, pressed his mouth against the man's ear, and whispered, "Do that again, I break your neck."

Wide-eyed, the man stared at Jake, a confused expression on his face. "Who are you, anyway?" he groaned.

"Just your luck, I'm a Texas Ranger."

Elizabeth watched from the end of the counter, the shock

beginning to fade. To Jake's surprise, she'd already gone after the gun. Legs spread, arms stiff, she held it straight out in both hands, pointing it at the robber.

Strong woman. She was an ex-Army wife, and it showed. Wouldn't she hate to hear that?

"Be careful with that thing," Jake said. "Don't shoot *me* by mistake."

Keeping her eyes riveted on the robber, she clipped the words out, "I know how to use it, and I will if I have to."

Her face and hair were wet with pieces of tomato. Jake swallowed. An icy tightness gripped his chest. She'd been that close to the bullet strike.

Jake nodded. "If he gets away from me and comes at you, fire and keep firing till he goes down." He turned to Tim Bailey, who stood behind the counter, speechless. "Call the sheriff, sir."

Bailey darted around the counter and out onto the sidewalk, hollering for help, yelling for the sheriff. Two male bystanders rushed into the store.

"Stay out!" Jake shouted.

"They're going after the sheriff now," Bailey said, panting. "Thank you, Jake. You saved my life."

∞

When they'd finished with Sheriff Morgan, Jake led Elizabeth to the buggy, helped her in, and shut the door behind her.

"That took forever," he said, slapping the reins.

Giving statements and completing paper work for the authorities took longer because the Frontier Battalion was involved and would want their statements. So would Fort Bliss.

A small crowd of onlookers stared and whispered among themselves in front of the store as Jake and Elizabeth pulled out into the street, leaving them behind.

The corners of his mouth dug in. He gave a long, grunting stretch. He was tired and his leg ached from hitting the floor with the gunman. He reached across the seat and took Elizabeth's hand, winding his fingers through hers. Her face was a chalky mask, and the small hand in his felt like a chunk of ice. "You look as washed out as I feel," he said.

"Everything happened so fast." She turned in her seat and stared at him. "You could easily have killed that man in the store, but you didn't."

She didn't miss a thing. "Wasn't necessary once I had him under control. It was better not to. I'm a Ranger and he's a civilian. And Mexican. That complicates things."

"And you didn't want me to see you do it."

He looked at her sharply.

"I was married to a soldier. I know what you're trained to do, Jake, so you don't have to shield me." She looked down at her fingers intertwined with his. "I guess your training came in handy today."

A smile pulled at his lips. "Starting to like my job, are you?"

"How do you stay so calm through everything? It's a little odd."

He gave a snort. "It took me years of practice to learn how. We're trained to handle emotions in tense situations. Detach and you stay in control. If you don't, you make mistakes. It's that simple." He paused. "You handled things pretty well yourself, by the way."

"You sound surprised."

He slid a glance at her. "Only because you looked so confident with that Colt in your hands. Who taught you how?" As soon as the question was out of his mouth, he wanted to call it back.

"Carl did."

Carl again.

He felt like breaking something.

Twenty-nine

"COME ON IN AND I'LL MAKE SOME COFFEE," Elizabeth said when they stopped at the Fort Bliss entrance gate. The guard recognized Jake and waved them through.

"Better not. You drink coffee this late, you'll be up all night."

A smile barely made it to her lips. "I probably will be anyway. Every time I close my eyes, I picture what happened at the store." She looked away. "I'm not used to being shot at, Jake."

One side of his mouth lifted. "Frankly, I don't like it much, either."

He followed her into the house, shut the door, and held his arms out. "Come here," he said.

She threw herself at him, wrapped her arms around his waist and hugged him as if she were drowning, her face flattened against his shirt. Her breath caught on a sob, and tears spread a warm, wet feeling across his chest.

"I was afraid I'd lost you, too." She pressed her mouth against his neck, the words coming out ragged.

He pulled her closer. She'd been worried about *him*.

A lump as hard as a peach pit swelled in his throat. He couldn't remember the last time anyone cried for him. A woman doesn't cry for a man unless she cares.

He blinked back tears as he held her tight. A heavy feeling overcame him as he thought back on everything she'd been through since the day her brother was murdered.

In the dim light of the narrow hall, they held each other— her crying, him soothing her. He'd never told her how he felt because he didn't quite believe it himself. Didn't *want* to believe that what he felt was love, because she wanted nothing to do with a man in the military.

Afraid I'd lost you, too.

If he was reading that right, she'd just told him she loved him.

A few moments later, she pushed away.

He looked at her. Her cheeks were wet. "You all right?" he asked.

Wiping at her eyes, she nodded. "I'm sorry. Don't pay any attention to me. Let me go wash this stuff out of my hair and get normal again. There's lemonade in the icebox if you don't want coffee."

He blew his breath out hard. "I really shouldn't stay. I've got paper work to do for Colonel Gordon. I don't want him taken by surprise. There will be questions in the morning from the sheriff. Will you be all right alone, or would you rather stay at my place? I'll sleep on the cot."

"You could stay here," she said.

They were stopped in front of her father's quarters at Fort Bliss.

He shook his head. "No, absolutely not. You're in the guest section here, and it's well patrolled. Everyone knows

266

you, and someone might have seen me come in. People are too quick to talk. Neither one of us needs the gossip. I'll be working on my reports till late into the night anyway. At Camp Annex, my quarters are off to themselves. Better for you."

"I'll come with you, then. I'm still shaky, which isn't like me. I guess I don't want to be alone tonight. I just need to gather a few things and get a clean outfit for tomorrow. I'll wash up at your house."

∽

Back at his quarters, Jake wandered into his small kitchen, set the oil lamp down, and went to the wooden icebox. Blankly he stared into its white interior at the everyday things of life: milk, pickles, biscuits, eggs. Cool air hit him in the face.

In the background, he heard water dripping. Elizabeth was in the other room, washing bits of tomato out of her hair.

His mind went back over the events of the day: the shooter at the store, Elizabeth's screaming. Just remembering made his throat go dry. If he'd stumbled on his run to the counter, if his kick had been a fraction off, if the gunman had been one second faster . . .

Dread screwed his eyes shut.

Nothing bothered him, she'd said.

She was wrong. Almost losing her today was a wake-up call. Just thinking about it now made it hard for him to get air into his lungs.

Most women would have ducked down behind that counter to save their own skin. Not Elizabeth. Instead, she had stepped in to save his. And he knew if the gunman, a bear of a man, had somehow gotten the upper hand, Elizabeth would've shot the man in an instant in order to save him.

He had Carl to thank for that.

His hand stilled as he stared into the icebox. Then the thought jumped into his mind: He had Carl to thank for a lot of things.

He slammed shut the icebox door and went into the living room to write up his report.

Every now and then, a smile crept onto his face. He stopped writing and ran a hand back and forth across his chest, feeling the damp front of his shirt—his cried-on shirt.

∞

At quarter past three in the morning, Jake shot bolt upright on the cot, his mouth dry again, his heart pounding in his ears. His back, his pillow, and the sheet beneath him were soaked with sweat. He sat up and swung his legs over the side, fighting through the fog in his head. A dream, a bad dream, that's all it was.

He shoved to his feet, rubbing his face with both hands, his mind still echoing with his own nightmarish screams. In his dream, she'd been killed.

Barefooted, he pulled on his trousers and went back into the living room.

Fully awake now, he sat down and tried to read over the report he'd written earlier. He leaned back in the chair. For someone as controlled as he was, when it came to Elizabeth, it was as if he were a different person altogether.

He couldn't concentrate. His mind jumped from one sentence to the other, not registering the words on the page.

He knew he wouldn't breathe easy until this thing was over and done with, the thief locked up behind bars.

A battle for another day.

∞

The next morning, wearing denim work pants, his hair still damp from washing, Jake brought Elizabeth coffee in his bed.

Her quiet, steady breathing told him she was still asleep. In the early morning light, her face seemed to glow. He stood there and gazed at her, at her lips relaxed in slumber. Softly, so as not to wake her, he leaned down and kissed her.

He looked into the shadows beyond the bed, his thoughts clear and sharp. Elizabeth stirred and sighed in her sleep. He gave one of his own and stepped back.

"Good mornin'," he said. "Time to get up."

She stretched and smiled at the coffee in his hand. He placed the steaming cup on the night table for her.

He leaned against the wall, deliberately not touching her, wanting no distractions until after he'd said what was on his mind. Arms folded across his chest, he wondered how to start.

"Why so serious?" she asked.

He was silent for a moment, his lips pursed.

"Last night was a wake-up call for me," he began. "For both of us."

She nodded, then asked quietly, "How long will you be here at Fort Bliss?"

"I'd like to work for Colonel Gordon, and then if I'm lucky, run a battalion of my own. A lot is happening in this country and in the Army. I'd like to be part of it. Then in five years or so, I could retire as a lieutenant colonel and—are you ready for this? Your father thinks I should get into his business. An ex-Army colonel would have a leg up. It's a big step for me. How long in Texas?" He shrugged. "The Army decides that."

"And if something else happens? What if there's another war?"

Jake's gaze held hers, steady, unwavering. "If that happens and I'm in the Army, I go in a heartbeat. You have to know that."

She swallowed. "What if something happens to you?"

He pushed off the wall and sat on the side of the bed, put his arm around her. "Unlike Rangers, colonels have a pretty good life expectancy. Their wives are important to their success as officers. But if something should happen, you say a prayer for me, and you deal with it, knowing I went doing something I believed in. Then you get on with your life. Nobody—military or civilian—can count on tomorrow. All we have for certain is today, right now."

"I thought about that last night."

"So did I." He squeezed her hand. "I want to spend all my todays with you. I love you, Elizabeth. Anything I do, I want you with me. Always. And although you might not want to, I think you love me, too."

She looked away without answering, then nodded and looked back at him. "I do."

Hearing that, he leaned down and kissed her on the lips. "Can I persuade you to say that in front of the chaplain?"

"Yes. And the sooner the better."

He smiled so wide, he thought his face would break.

"Let's go tell Ruthie," he said.

Thirty

THE WEDDING AND FESTIVITIES surrounding the happy event was everything Elizabeth had dreamed about. For Jake's sake, she asked for a military wedding—traditional, formal, and beautiful. It seemed as though half of El Paso had come out to Fort Bliss to see Lloyd's little sister marry a handsome Cavalry major.

The ceremony was conducted by Jake's friend, Army Chaplain William Tyler. Suzanne was maid of honor, and brand-new Lieutenant Gus Dukker was the best man.

The recessional under the arch of swords was both dramatic and humorous. Elizabeth, her ivory wedding gown trailing on the carpet, giggled when the last swordsman tapped her fanny with his sword as she went by. "Welcome to the U.S. Army, ma'am," he said.

∞

Nearly every week, the telegraph at Elizabeth's office chattered with a message about General Diego's trial. The *Grande Examiner* kept its readers informed of the progress—both of the admired Mexican President Hector Guevara and of the trial proceedings in the U.S. for the Mexican rogue general.

General Diego and Major Chavez had been transferred under heavy guard to an unnamed Federal installation in East Texas where they were awaiting trial.

As expected—or perhaps it was privately agreed upon—Mexico was leaving the entire matter up to the United States. President Guevara was solidifying his position daily. He still kept military guards along Chihuahua's rivers to protect the dams, but nothing out of the ordinary had happened.

Time and again, Jake, Gus, Fred, and Elizabeth took the train to Austin for the hearings. Each time, their appearance in court was accompanied by a throng of reporters from the press. Although Elizabeth was nervous about testifying at first, Jake was calm and relaxed. He was no stranger to hearings and giving testimony. That went along with being a Ranger and a lawman.

Elizabeth had never seen him in a suit before and was impressed at how official he looked at the legislative meetings her father dragged him to. Jake's interests centered on security for the lawmakers and state officials, bringing in extra protection when necessary, even at small community meetings.

∞

After a packed final sentencing in Austin—at which time General Diego and Major Chavez both drew lifelong prison sentences for the death of Lloyd Madison, and a list of victims going back three years—a barbecue was announced for that evening.

Each time they were called to Austin, they were expected to attend one of these shindigs, entertained as honored guests. Senator Madison came several times, as Jake's guest, accompanying them to the parties and barbecues that followed the testimony.

Jake had reservations about attending. "I'm glad it's over, but celebrating prison sentences somehow strikes me as wrong."

Elizabeth nodded and looked for a polite escape.

Frank and Gus wanted to stay for the down-home, boot-stomping Texas blowout, hosted by Senator Elmore Carter and his pretty Mexican wife, Margarita.

Loud country-western music sounded from the terrace of the stately stone mansion outside Austin.

Jake would just as soon have bypassed all the social events until Senator Madison explained what was really going on. Jake was being looked at for something else.

Whatever it was, Jake wasn't sure he wanted it.

When he'd accepted Colonel Gordon's invitation to come back to the Fourth Cavalry, it had felt like coming home to him. He wore the gold leaves of Major easily and liked running the battalion the way Colonel Gordon wanted.

Jake checked his pocket watch and asked Elizabeth how long before they could decently leave. She pulled him aside to where they could speak privately.

"I know, I know," he said. "Your dad insists it's leading to something more for me. For us. Something political. But this is your kind of crowd, not mine. I'm a soldier, not a statesman. I'd be nothing here without you."

Elizabeth laughed and hugged his arm close. "If that's what you think, you are so wrong." She turned. "I'll be right back. I want to tell Dad good-bye," she called over her shoulder.

A big dark-haired man in denims and boots—Texas State Senator Max Roberts—saw Jake and walked over, hand outstretched.

"Howdy there, Major Nelson. Glad you could make it," he said, a hint of his Yale accent slipping through.

Jake walked to meet him and grabbed his hand. Normally, Jake was weary of the pretense, except this man he especially liked.

"I heard talk the Army's sending you another battalion to get ready," Roberts said quietly.

"Looks that way." Jake shook his head. "I've got to get this present one ready to go before that can happen."

"We need men like you in public office—strong, ethical men who love Texas and can see the big picture. The legislature's going to have a Senate opening in a couple of years. Assuming your battalion falls into place for you, would you consider leaving the Army to run for office?"

Jake studied Max Roberts. What he was intimating was something that fit Jake's own personal schedule. The Army first, and then the law.

"I've thought about it," Jake said, "but I felt committed to the military first. Then there'd be time for me." He paused, then said, "I'll need some help."

"You'll have all you need. Some powerful men have been watching you, and they like what they see," Roberts said. "I've been appointed to sound you out. I have to be in El Paso next Wednesday and Thursday. Let's talk about it then."

Max Roberts looked up. "And here comes your pretty wife. I'll go back to mine now." He threw an arm around

Jake's shoulder. "I want you to know I'm looking forward to next week."

Jake watched Roberts heading back to the party and grinned.

Senator Jake Nelson.

Had kind of a nice ring to it.

Acknowledgments

Many thanks to Rachel Murphree, Borderlands librarian at El Paso Community College, who knows so much about the Texas Rangers.

Thanks also to Jim Ryan who provided information about the Texas Rangers. A dedicated historian for Ranger and Indian Wars, Jim provided helpful details for the novel. For those readers who may be interested, visit his website at *fbtre.org*.

Thanks to Ken Prusso, the great-great-great nephew of a famous Texas Ranger, William Alexander Wallace, known as Bigfoot Wallace. Ken's stories about his uncle bring those long-ago Ranger heroes to life. "Bigfoot" was six feet two inches tall—and was the runt of his family.

Thanks to "Cowboy Bob" Lemen, a former Minnesota state legislator, writer, amateur historian, and horseman, who helped vet some of the details in this book. His website, *lemen.com*, has lots of insights into good horsemanship and Old West history.

Thanks to Christina Stopka, Deputy Director, Texas Ranger Hall of Fame and Museum. She always knew where to find the information on the Frontier Battalion needed for the story.

Thanks to James Smith, Librarian, U.S. Cavalry Association, for the information he provided on the Cavalry and their weapons.

Thanks also to CW4 Tom Callahan, U.S. Army Retired, for his insight and information about the American military. Tom always had the answers—or knew where to get them for the story.

Thanks to Mary Sue Seymour for unfailingly good advice.

And a special thanks to my editors, David Long and Luke Hinrichs, two gentlemen this writer was lucky to have in her corner. Their encouragement and support made all the difference.

About the Author

Yvonne Harris earned a Bachelor of Science degree in education from the University of Hartford and has taught throughout New England and the mid-Atlantic. Currently she teaches writing at a local college. She is a winner and three-time finalist of the Golden Heart Award. Before turning to fiction, she wrote articles for magazines. Although Yvonne and her husband live in New Jersey to be close to family, she was raised in Alabama and considers herself a Southern writer.

More Texas Adventure and Romance

She thinks he's arrogant. He thinks she's vain. Yet they have one thing in common: They are both completely wrong...and completely right for each other.

A Tailor-Made Bride by Karen Witemeyer

When Adelaide Proctor, a recovering romantic, goes to work for a handsome Texas ranch owner, her heart's not the only thing in danger!

Head in the Clouds by Karen Witemeyer

Eden Spencer prefers her books over suitors. But when a tarnished hero captures her heart, will she deny her feelings or create her own love story?

To Win Her Heart by Karen Witemeyer

Touching Historical Romance from
Delia Parr

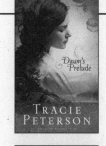